Dear Reader,

There has never been a magical kingdom quite like Oz. Populated by good witches and wicked witches, wretched Nomes and enchanting princesses, chattering hens and cowardly lions—a whole host of marvelous creatures great and small and wise and wonderful—Oz is one of the most beloved fantasy worlds ever created.

The enormous explosion of all types of fantasy that we are seeing in today's market makes us feel that now is the time for a brilliantly successful Oz revival.

When we mention Oz to people who haven't grown up with the books, they nod, mention Judy Garland and think they know all there is to know about Oz. How wrong they are! They have no idea how rich the series is, how many wonderful characters and creatures there are. We have every expectation of making Oz as familiar to millions of fantasy readers as is Tolkien's Middle-earth and Lewis's Narnia.

Del Rey Books is now publishing the first seven books in the series, with more to follow.

Come, join us in Oz.

Magically,
Judy-Lynn & Lester del Rey
Del Rey Books

 **IS ...**

"Oz—where the young stay young and the old grow young forever—these books are for readers of all ages."

—Ray Bradbury

"Who says the Land of Oz is only for the young? Age has nothing to do with it. Oz belongs to the young at heart and always will. All that is needed is an adventuresome spirit and a genuine affection for classic fantasy."

—Terry Brooks
Author of *The Sword of Shannara*

"I was raised with the Oz books, and their enchantment, humor and excitement remain with me. They are still a joy and a treasure. I welcome this Oz revival."

—Stephen R. Donaldson
Author of *The Chronicles of Thomas Covenant*

"The land of Oz has managed to fascinate each new generation . . . the Oz books continue to exert their spell . . . and those who read [them] are often made what they were not—imaginative, tolerant, alert to wonders, life."

—Gore Vidal
The New York Review of Books

This Book
Belongs to

The Wonderful Oz Books by L. Frank Baum
Now Published by Del Rey Books

THE EMERALD CITY OF OZ

BY

L. FRANK BAUM

Author of The Road to Oz, Dorothy and The
Wizard in Oz, The Land of Oz, etc.

ILLUSTRATED BY

JOHN R. NEILL

A Del Rey Book

BALLANTINE BOOKS • NEW YORK

A Del Rey Book
Published by Ballantine Book

Library of Congress Catalog Card Number: 79-88481

ISBN 0-345-32028-X

This edition published by arrangement with Contemporary
Books, Inc.

Manufactured in the United States of America

First Ballantine Books Edition: November 1979
Third Printing: May 1985

Cover art by Michael Herring

TO
HER ROYAL HIGHNESS
CYNTHIA II
OF SYRACUSE,
AND TO EACH AND EVERY ONE
OF THE CHILDREN WHOSE LOYAL
APPRECIATION HAS ENCOURAGED
ME TO WRITE THE OZ BOOKS
THIS VOLUME IS AFFECTIONATELY
DEDICATED.

OZMA

DOROTHY

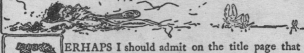

ERHAPS I should admit on the title page that this book is "By L. Frank Baum and his correspondents," for I have used many suggestions conveyed to me in letters from children. Once on a time I really imagined myself "an author of fairy tales," but now I am merely an editor or private secretary for a host of youngsters whose ideas I am requested to weave into the thread of my stories.

These ideas are often clever. They are also logical and interesting. So I have used them whenever I could find an opportunity, and it is but just that I acknowledge my indebtedness to my little friends.

My, what imaginations these children have developed! Sometimes I am fairly astounded by their daring and genius. There will be no lack of fairy-tale authors in the future, I am sure. My readers have told me what to do with Dorothy, and Aunt Em and Uncle Henry, and I have obeyed their mandates. They have also given me a variety of subjects to write about in the future: enough, in fact, to keep me busy for some time. I am very proud of this alliance. Children love these stories because children have helped to create them. My readers know what they want and realize that I try to please them. The result is very satisfactory to the publishers, to me, and (I am quite sure) to the children.

I hope, my dears, it will be a long time before we are obliged to dissolve partnership.

Coronado, 1910   L. FRANK BAUM.

LIST OF CHAPTERS

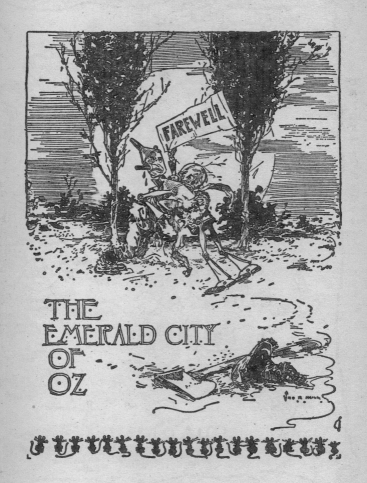

THE EMERALD CITY OF OZ

How the Nome King Became Angry

CHAPTER ONE

THE Nome King was in an angry mood, and at such times he was very disagreeable. Every one kept away from him, even his Chief Steward Kaliko.

Therefore the King stormed and raved all by himself, walking up and down in his jewel-studded cavern and getting angrier all the time. Then he remembered that it was no fun being angry unless he had some one to frighten and make miserable, and he rushed to his big gong and made it clatter as loud as he could.

In came the Chief Steward, trying not to show the Nome King how frightened he was.

"Send the Chief Counselor here!" shouted the angry monarch.

Kaliko ran out as fast as his spindle legs could carry his fat round body, and soon the Chief

I

Counselor entered the cavern. The King scowled and said to him:

"I'm in great trouble over the loss of my Magic Belt. Every little while I want to do something magical, and find I can't because the Belt is gone. That makes me angry, and when I'm angry I can't have a good time. Now, what do you advise?"

"Some people," said the Chief Counselor, "enjoy getting angry."

"But not all the time," declared the King. "To be angry once in a while is really good fun, because it makes others so miserable. But to be angry morning, noon and night, as I am, grows monotonous and prevents my gaining any other pleasure in life. Now, what do you advise?"

"Why, if you are angry because you want to do magical things and can't, and if you don't want to get angry at all, my advice is not to want to do magical things."

Hearing this, the King glared at his Counselor with a furious expression and tugged at his own long white whiskers until he pulled them so hard that he yelled with pain.

"You are a fool!" he exclaimed.

"I share that honor with your Majesty," said the Chief Counselor.

The King roared with rage and stamped his foot.

"Ho, there, my guards!" he cried. "Ho" is a royal way of saying, "Come here." So, when the guards had hoed, the King said to them:

"Take this Chief Counselor and throw him away."

Then the guards took the Chief Counselor, and bound him with chains to prevent his struggling, and threw him away. And the King paced up and down his cavern more angry than before.

Finally he rushed to his big gong and made it clatter like a fire-alarm. Kaliko appeared again, trembling and white with fear.

"Fetch my pipe!" yelled the King.

"Your pipe is already here, your Majesty," replied Kaliko.

"Then get my tobacco!" roared the King.

"The tobacco is in your pipe, your Majesty," returned the Steward.

"Then bring a live coal from the furnace!" commanded the King.

"The tobacco is lighted, and your Majesty is already smoking your pipe," answered the Steward.

"Why, so I am!" said the King, who had forgotten this fact; "but you are very rude to remind me of it."

"I am a lowborn, miserable villain," declared the Chief Steward, humbly.

The Nome King could think of nothing to say next, so he puffed away at his pipe and paced up and down the room. Finally he remembered how angry he was, and cried out:

"What do you mean, Kaliko, by being so contented when your monarch is unhappy?"

"What makes you unhappy?" asked the Steward.

"I've lost my Magic Belt. A little girl named Dorothy, who was here with Ozma of Oz, stole my Belt and carried it away with her," said the King, grinding his teeth with rage.

"She captured it in a fair fight," Kaliko ventured to say.

"But I want it! I must have it! Half my power is gone with that Belt!" roared the King.

"You will have to go to the Land of Oz to recover it, and your Majesty can't get to the Land of Oz in any possible way," said the Steward, yawning because he had been on duty ninety-six hours, and was sleepy.

"Why not?" asked the King.

"Because there is a deadly desert all around that fairy country, which no one is able to cross. You know that fact as well as I do, your Majesty. Never mind the lost Belt. You have plenty of power left, for you rule this underground kingdom like a tyrant, and thousands of Nomes obey your commands. I advise you to drink a glass of melted silver, to quiet your nerves, and then go to bed."

The King grabbed a big ruby and threw it at Kaliko's head. The Steward ducked to escape the heavy jewel, which crashed against the door just over his left ear.

"Get out of my sight! Vanish! Go away—and send General Blug here," screamed the Nome King.

Kaliko hastily withdrew, and the Nome King stamped up and down until the General of his armies appeared.

This Nome was known far and wide as a terrible fighter and a cruel, desperate commander. He had fifty thousand Nome soldiers, all well drilled, who feared nothing but their stern master. Yet General Blug was a trifle uneasy when he arrived and saw how angry the Nome King was.

"Ha! So you're here!" cried the King.

"So I am," said the General.

"March your army at once to the Land of Oz, capture and destroy the Emerald City, and bring back to me my Magic Belt!" roared the King.

"You're crazy," calmly remarked the General.

"What's that? What's that? What's that?" And the Nome King danced around on his pointed toes, he was so enraged.

"You don't know what you're talking about," continued the General, seating himself upon a large cut diamond. "I advise you to stand in a corner and count sixty before you speak again. By that time you may be more sensible."

The King looked around for something to to throw at General Blug, but as nothing was handy he began to consider that perhaps the man was right and he had been talking foolishly. So he merely threw himself into his glittering throne and tipped his crown over his ear and curled his feet up under him and glared wickedly at Blug.

"In the first place," said the General, "we cannot march across the deadly desert to the Land of Oz; and, if we could, the Ruler of that country, Princess Ozma, has certain fairy powers that would render my army helpless. Had you not lost your Magic Belt we might have some chance of defeating Ozma; but the Belt is gone."

"I want it!" screamed the King. "I must have it."

"Well, then, let us try in a sensible way to get it," replied the General. "The Belt was captured by a little girl named Dorothy, who lives in Kansas, in the United States of America."

7

"But she left it in the Emerald City, with Ozma," declared the King.

"How do you know that?" asked the General.

"One of my spies, who is a Blackbird, flew over the desert to the Land of Oz, and saw the Magic Belt in Ozma's palace," replied the King with a groan.

"Now, that gives me an idea," said General Blug, thoughtfully. "There are two ways to get

to the Land of Oz without traveling across the sandy desert."

"What are they?" demanded the King, eagerly.

"One way is *over* the desert, through the air; and the other way is *under* the desert, through the earth."

Hearing this the Nome King uttered a yell

of joy and leaped from his throne, to resume his wild walk up and down the cavern.

"That's it, Blug!" he shouted. "That's the idea, General! I'm King of the Under World, and my subjects are all miners. I'll make a secret tunnel under the desert to the Land of Oz—yes! right up to the Emerald City—and you will march your armies there and capture the whole country!"

"Softly, softly, your Majesty. Don't go too fast," warned the General. "My Nomes are good fighters, but they are not strong enough to conquer the Emerald City."

"Are you sure?" asked the King.

"Absolutely certain, your Majesty."

"Then what am I to do?"

"Give up the idea and mind your own business," advised the General. "You have plenty to do trying to rule your underground kingdom."

"But I want that Magic Belt—and I'm going to have it!" roared the Nome King.

"I'd like to see you get it," replied the General, laughing maliciously.

The King was by this time so exasperated that he picked up his scepter, which had a heavy ball, made from a sapphire, at the end of it, and threw it with all his force at General Blug. The sapphire hit the General upon his forehead and knocked him flat upon the ground, where he lay motionless. Then the King rang his gong and told his guards to drag out the General and throw him away; which they did.

This Nome King was named Roquat the Red, and no one loved him. He was a bad man and a powerful monarch, and he had resolved to destroy the Land of Oz and its magnificent Emerald City, to enslave Princess Ozma and little Dorothy and all the Oz people, and recover his Magic Belt. This same Belt had once enabled

Roquat the Red to carry out many wicked plans; but that was before Ozma and her people marched to the underground cavern and captured it. The Nome King could not forgive Dorothy or Princess Ozma, and he had determined to be revenged upon them.

But they, for their part, did not know they had so dangerous an enemy. Indeed, Ozma and Dorothy had both almost forgotten that such a person as the Nome King yet lived under the mountains of the Land of Ev—which lay just across the deadly desert to the south of the Land of Oz.

An unsuspected enemy is doubly dangerous.

How UNCLE HENRY GOT INTO TROUBLE

CHAPTER TWO

DOROTHY GALE lived on a farm in Kansas, with her Aunt Em and her Uncle Henry. It was not a big farm, nor a very good one, because sometimes the rain did not come when the crops needed it, and then everything withered and dried up. Once a cyclone had carried away Uncle Henry's house, so that he was obliged to build another; and as he was a poor man he had to mortgage his farm to get the money to pay for the new house. Then his health became bad and he was too feeble to work. The doctor ordered him to take a sea voyage and he went to Australia and took Dorothy with him. That cost a lot of money, too.

Uncle Henry grew poorer every year, and the crops raised on the farm only bought food for the family. Therefore the mortgage could not be paid. At last the banker who had loaned him the money said that if he did not pay on a certain day, his farm would be taken away from him.

This worried Uncle Henry a good deal, for without the farm he would have no way to earn a living. He was a good man, and worked in the fields as hard as he could; and Aunt Em did all the housework, with Dorothy's help. Yet they did not seem to get along.

This little girl, Dorothy, was like dozens of little girls you know. She was loving and usually sweet-tempered, and had a round rosy face and earnest eyes. Life was a serious thing to Dorothy, and a wonderful thing, too, for she had encountered more strange adventures in her short life than many other girls of her age.

Aunt Em once said she thought the fairies must have marked Dorothy at her birth, because she had wandered into strange places and had always been protected by some unseen power. As for Uncle Henry, he thought his little niece merely a dreamer, as her dead mother had been, for he could not quite believe all the curious stories Dorothy told them of the Land of Oz, which she had several times visited. He did not think that she tried to deceive her uncle and aunt, but he imagined that she had dreamed all of those astonishing adventures, and that the dreams had been so real to her that she had come to believe them true.

Whatever the explanation might be, it was certain that Dorothy had been absent from her Kansas home for several long periods, always disappearing unexpectedly, yet always coming back safe and sound, with amazing tales of where she had been and the unusual people she had met. Her uncle and aunt listened to her stories eagerly and in spite of their doubts began to feel that the little girl had gained a lot of experience and wisdom that were unaccountable in this age, when fairies are supposed no longer to exist.

Most of Dorothy's stories were about the Land of Oz, with its beautiful Emerald City and a lovely girl Ruler named Ozma, who was the most faithful friend of the little Kansas girl. When Dorothy told about the riches of this fairy country Uncle Henry would sigh, for he knew that a single one of the great emeralds that were so common there would pay all his debts and leave his farm free. But Dorothy never brought any jewels home with her, so their poverty became greater every year.

When the banker told Uncle Henry that he must pay the money in thirty days or leave the farm, the poor man was in despair, as he knew he could not possibly get the money. So he told his wife, Aunt Em, of his trouble, and she first cried a little and then said that they must be brave and do the best they could, and go away somewhere and try to earn an honest living. But they were getting old and feeble and she feared that they could not take care of Dorothy as well as they had formerly done. Probably the little girl would also be obliged to go to work.

They did not tell their niece the sad news for several days, not wishing to make her unhappy; but one morning the little girl found Aunt Em softly crying while Uncle Henry tried to comfort her. Then Dorothy asked them to tell her what was the matter.

"We must give up the farm, my dear," replied her uncle, sadly, "and wander away into the world to work for our living."

The girl listened quite seriously, for she had not known before how desperately poor they were.

"We don't mind for ourselves," said her aunt, stroking the little girl's head tenderly; "but we love you as if you were our own child, and we are heart-broken to think that you must also endure poverty, and work for a living before you have grown big and strong."

"What could I do to earn money?" asked Dorothy.

"You might do housework for some one, dear, you are so handy; or perhaps you could be a nurse-maid to little children. I'm sure I don't know exactly what you *can* do to earn money, but if your uncle and I are able to support you we will do it willingly, and send you to school. We fear, though, that we shall have much trouble in earning a living for ourselves. No one wants to employ old people who are broken down in health, as we are."

Dorothy smiled.

"Wouldn't it be funny," she said, "for me to do housework in Kansas, when I'm a Princess in the Land of Oz?"

"A Princess!" they both exclaimed, astonished.

"Yes; Ozma made me a Princess some time ago, and she has often begged me to come and live always in the Emerald City," said the child.

Her uncle and aunt looked at each other in amazement. Then the man said:

"Do you suppose you could manage to return to your fairyland, my dear?"

"Oh, yes," replied Dorothy; "I could do that easily."

"How?" asked Aunt Em.

"Ozma sees me every day at four o'clock, in her Magic Picture. She can see me wherever I am, no matter what I am doing. And at that time, if I make a certain secret sign, she will send for me by means of the Magic Belt, which I once captured from the Nome King. Then, in the wink of an eye, I shall be with Ozma in her palace."

The elder people remained silent for some time after Dorothy had spoken. Finally Aunt Em said, with another sigh of regret:

"If that is the case, Dorothy, perhaps you'd better go and live in the Emerald City. It will break our hearts to lose you from our lives, but you will be so much better off with your fairy friends that it seems wisest and best for you to go."

"I'm not so sure about that," remarked Uncle Henry, shaking his gray head doubtfully. "These things all seem real to Dorothy, I know; but I'm afraid our little girl won't find her fairyland just what she has dreamed it to be. It would make me very unhappy to think that she was wandering among strangers who might be unkind to her."

Dorothy laughed merrily at this speech, and then she became very sober again, for she could see how all this trouble was worrying her aunt and uncle, and knew that unless she found a way to help them their future lives would be quite miserable and unhappy. She knew that she *could* help them. She had thought of a way already. Yet she did not tell them at once what it was, because she must ask Ozma's consent before she would be able to carry out her plans.

So she only said:

"If you will promise not to worry a bit about me, I'll go to the Land of Oz this very afternoon. And I'll make a promise, too; that you shall both see me again before the day comes when you must leave this farm."

"The day isn't far away, now," her uncle sadly replied. "I did not tell you of our trouble until I was obliged to, dear Dorothy, so the evil time is near at hand. But if you are quite sure your fairy friends will give you a home, it will be best for you to go to them, as your aunt says."

That was why Dorothy went to her little room in the attic that afternoon, taking with her a small dog named Toto. The dog had curly black hair and big brown eyes and loved Dorothy very dearly.

The child had kissed her uncle and aunt affectionately before she went upstairs, and now she looked around her little room rather wistfully, gazing at the simple trinkets and worn calico and gingham dresses, as if they were old friends. She was tempted at first to make a bundle of them, yet she knew very well that they would be of no use to her in her future life.

She sat down upon a broken-backed chair—the only one the room contained—and holding

Toto in her arms waited patiently until the clock struck four.

Then she made the secret signal that had been agreed upon between her and Ozma.

Uncle Henry and Aunt Em waited downstairs. They were uneasy and a good deal excited, for this is a practical humdrum world, and it seemed to them quite impossible that their little niece could vanish from her home and travel instantly to fairyland.

So they watched the stairs, which seemed to be the only way that Dorothy could get out of the farmhourse, and they watched them a long time. They heard the clock strike four but there was no sound from above.

Half-past four came, and now they were too impatient to wait any longer. Softly they crept

up the stairs to the door of the little girl's room.
"Dorothy! Dorothy!" they called.
There was no answer.
They opened the door and looked in.
The room was empty.

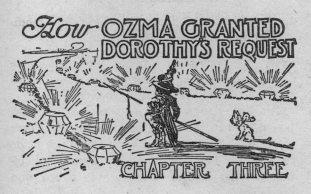

How OZMA GRANTED DOROTHY'S REQUEST

CHAPTER THREE

I SUPPOSE you have read so much about the magnificent Emerald City that there is little need for me to describe it here. It is the Capital City of the Land of Oz, which is justly considered the most attractive and delightful fairyland in all the world.

The Emerald City is built all of beautiful marbles in which are set a profusion of emeralds, every one exquisitely cut and of very great size. There are other jewels used in the decorations inside the houses and palaces, such as rubies, diamonds, sapphires, amethysts and turquoises. But in the streets and upon the outside of the buildings only emeralds appear, from which circumstance the place is named the Emerald City of Oz. It has nine thousand, six hundred and fifty-four buildings, in which lived fifty-seven thousand three hundred and eighteen people, up to the time my story opens.

All the surrounding country, extending to the borders of the desert which enclosed it upon every side, was full of pretty and comfortable farmhouses, in which resided those inhabitants of Oz who preferred country to city life.

Altogether there were more than half a million people in the Land of Oz—although some of them, as you will soon learn, were not made of flesh and blood as we are—and every inhabitant of that favored country was happy and prosperous.

No disease of any sort was ever known among the Ozites, and so no one ever died unless he met with an accident that prevented him from living. This happened very seldom, indeed. There were no poor people in the Land of Oz, because there was no such thing as money, and all property of every sort belonged to the Ruler. The people were her children, and she cared for them. Each person was given freely by his neighbors whatever he required for his use, which is as much as any one may reasonably desire. Some tilled the lands and raised great crops of grain, which was divided equally among the entire population, so that all had enough. There were many tailors and dressmakers and shoemakers and the like, who made things that any who desired them might wear. Likewise there were jewelers who made ornaments for the person, which pleased and beautified the people, and these ornaments also were free to those who asked for them. Each man and woman, no matter what he or she produced for the good of the community, was supplied by the neighbors with food and clothing and a house and furniture and ornaments and games. If by chance the supply ever ran short, more was taken from the great storehouses of the Ruler, which were afterward filled up again when there was more of any article than the people needed.

Every one worked half the time and played half the time, and the people enjoyed the work as much as they did the play, because it is good to be occupied and to have something to do. There were no cruel overseers set to watch them, and no one to rebuke them or to find fault with them. So each one was proud to do all he could for his friends and neighbors, and was glad when they would accept the things he produced.

You will know, by what I have here told you, that the Land of Oz was a remarkable country. I do not suppose such an arrangement would be practical with us, but Dorothy assures me that it works finely with the Oz people.

Oz being a fairy country, the people were, of course, fairy people; but that does not mean that all of them were very unlike the people of our own world. There were all sorts of queer characters among them, but not a single one who was evil, or who possessed a selfish or violent nature. They were peaceful, kind-hearted, loving and merry, and every inhabitant adored the beautiful girl who ruled them, and delighted to obey her every command.

In spite of all I have said in a general way, there were some parts of the Land of Oz not quite so pleasant as the farming country and the Emerald City which was its center. Far away in the South Country there lived in the mountains a band of strange people called Hammer-Heads, because they had no arms and used their flat heads to pound any one who came near them. Their necks were like rubber, so that they could shoot out their heads to quite a distance, and afterward draw them back again to their shoulders. The Hammer-Heads were called the "Wild People," but never harmed any but those who disturbed them in the mountains where they lived.

In some of the dense forests there lived great beasts of every sort; yet these were for the most part harmless and even sociable, and conversed agreeably with those who visited their haunts. The Kalidahs—beasts with bodies like bears and heads like tigers—had once been fierce and bloodthirsty, but even they were now nearly all tamed, although at times one or another of them would get cross and disagreeable.

Not so tame were the Fighting Trees, which had a forest of their own. If any one approached them these curious trees would bend down their branches, twine them around the intruders, and hurl them away.

But these unpleasant things existed only in a few remote parts of the Land of Oz. I suppose every country has some drawbacks, so even this almost perfect fairyland could not be quite perfect. Once there had been wicked witches in the land, too; but now these had all been destroyed; so, as I said, only peace and happiness reigned in Oz.

For some time Ozma has ruled over this fair country, and never was Ruler more popular or beloved. She is said to be the most beautiful girl the world has ever known, and her heart and mind are as lovely as her person.

Dorothy Gale had several times visited the Emerald City and experienced adventures in the Land of Oz, so that she and Ozma had now become firm friends. The girl Ruler had even made Dorothy a Princess of Oz, and had often implored her to come to Ozma's stately palace and live there always; but Dorothy had been loyal to her Aunt Em and Uncle Henry, who had cared for her since she was a baby, and she had refused to leave them because she knew they would be lonely without her.

However, Dorothy now realized that things were going to be different with her uncle and aunt from this time forth, so after giving the matter deep thought she decided to ask Ozma to grant her a very great favor.

A few seconds after she had made the secret signal in her little bedchamber, the Kansas girl was seated in a lovely room in Ozma's palace in the Emerald City of Oz. When the first loving kisses and embraces had been exchanged, the fair Ruler inquired:

"What is the matter, dear? I know something unpleasant has happened to you, for your face was very sober when I saw it in my Magic Picture. And whenever you signal me to transport you to this safe place, where you are always welcome, I know you are in danger or in trouble."

Dorothy sighed.

"This time, Ozma, it isn't I," she replied. "But it's worse, I guess, for Uncle Henry and Aunt Em are in a heap of trouble, and there seems no way for them to get out of it—anyhow, not while they live in Kansas."

"Tell me about it, Dorothy," said Ozma, with ready sympathy.

"Why, you see Uncle Henry is poor; for the

farm in Kansas doesn't 'mount to much, as farms go. So one day Uncle Henry borrowed some money, and wrote a letter saying that if he didn't pay the money back they could take his farm for pay. Course he 'spected to pay by making money from the farm; but he just couldn't. An' so they're going to take the farm, and Uncle Henry and Aunt Em won't have any place to live. They're pretty old to do much hard work, Ozma; so I'll have to work for them, unless—"

Ozma had been thoughtful during the story, but now she smiled and pressed her little friend's hand.

"Unless what, dear?" she asked.

Dorothy hesitated, because her request meant so much to them all.

"Well," said she, "I'd like to live here in the Land of Oz, where you've often 'vited me to live. But I can't, you know, unless Uncle Henry and Aunt Em could live here too."

"Of course not," exclaimed the Ruler of Oz, laughing gaily. "So, in order to get you, little friend, we must invite your Uncle and Aunt to live in Oz, also."

"Oh, will you, Ozma?" cried Dorothy, clasping her chubby little hands eagerly. "Will you bring them here with the Magic Belt, and give them a nice little farm in the Munchkin Coun-

27

try, or the Winkie Country—or some other place?"

"To be sure," answered Ozma, full of joy at the chance to please her little friend. "I have long been thinking of this very thing, Dorothy dear, and often I have had it in my mind to propose it to you. I am sure your uncle and aunt must be good and worthy people, or you would not love them so much; and for *your* friends, Princess, there is always room in the Land of Oz."

Dorothy was delighted, yet not altogether surprised, for she had clung to the hope that Ozma would be kind enough to grant her request. When, indeed, had her powerful and faithful friend refused her anything?

"But you must not call me 'Princess,'" she said; "for after this I shall live on the little farm with Uncle Henry and Aunt Em, and princesses ought not to live on farms."

"Princess Dorothy will not," replied Ozma, with her sweet smile. "You are going to live in your own rooms in this palace, and be my constant companion."

"But Uncle Henry—" began Dorothy.

"Oh, he is old, and has worked enough in his lifetime," interrupted the girl Ruler; "so we must find a place for your uncle and aunt where they will be comfortable and happy and need not work more than they care to. When shall we transport them here, Dorothy?"

"I promised to go and see them again before they were turned out of the farmhouse," answered Dorothy; "so—perhaps next Saturday—"

"But why wait so long?" asked Ozma. "And why make the journey back to Kansas again? Let us surprise them, and bring them here without any warning."

"I'm not sure that they believe in the Land of Oz," said Dorothy, "though I've told 'em 'bout it lots of times."

"They'll believe when they see it," declared Ozma; "and if they are told they are to make a magical journey to our fairyland, it may make them nervous. I think the best way will be to use the Magic Belt without warning them, and when they have arrived you can explain to them whatever they do not understand."

"Perhaps that's best," decided Dorothy. "There isn't much use in their staying at the farm until they are put out, 'cause it's much nicer here."

"Then to-morrow morning they shall come here," said Princess Ozma. "I will order Jellia Jamb, who is the palace housekeeper, to have rooms all prepared for them, and after breakfast we will get the Magic Belt and by its aid transport your uncle and aunt to the Emerald City."

"Thank you, Ozma!" cried Dorothy, kissing her friend gratefully.

"And now," Ozma proposed, "let us take a walk in the gardens before we dress for dinner. Come, Dorothy dear!"

How THE NOME KING PLANNED REVENGE

CHAPTER FOUR

THE reason most people are bad is because they do not try to be good. Now, the Nome King had never tried to be good, so he was very bad indeed. Having decided to conquer the Land of Oz and to destroy the Emerald City and enslave all its people, King Roquat the Red kept planning ways to do this dreadful thing, and the more he planned the more he believed he would be able to accomplish it.

About the time Dorothy went to Ozma the Nome King called his Chief Steward to him and said:

"Kaliko, I think I shall make you the General of my armies."

"I think you won't," replied Kaliko, positively.

"Why not?" inquired the King, reaching for his scepter with the big sapphire.

"Because I'm your Chief Steward, and know nothing of warfare," said Kaliko, preparing to dodge if anything were thrown at him. "I manage all the affairs of your kingdom better than you could yourself, and you'll never find another Steward as good as I am. But there are a hundred Nomes better fitted to command your army, and your Generals get thrown away so often that I have no desire to be one of them."

"Ah, there is some truth in your remarks, Kaliko," remarked the King, deciding not to throw the scepter. "Summon my army to assemble in the Great Cavern."

Kaliko bowed and retired, and in a few minutes returned to say that the army was assembled. So the King went out upon a balcony that overlooked the Great Cavern, where fifty thousand Nomes, all armed with swords and pikes, stood marshaled in military array.

When they were not required as soldiers all these Nomes were metal workers and miners, and they had hammered so much at the forges and dug so hard with pick and shovel that they had acquired great muscular strength. They were strangely formed creatures, rather round and not very tall. Their toes were curly and their ears broad and flat.

In time of war every Nome left his forge or mine and became part of the great army of King

Roquat. The soldiers wore rock-colored uniforms and were excellently drilled.

The King looked upon this tremendous army, which stood silently arrayed before him, and a cruel smile curled the corners of his mouth, for he saw that his legions were very powerful. Then he addressed them from the balcony, saying:

"I have thrown away General Blug, because he did not please me. So I want another General to command this army. Who is next in command?"

"I am," replied Colonel Crinkle, a dapper-looking Nome, as he stepped forward to salute his monarch.

The King looked at him carefully and said:

"I want you to march this army through an underground tunnel, which I am going to bore, to the Emerald City of Oz. When you get there I want you to conquer the Oz people, destroy them and their city, and bring all their gold and silver and precious stones back to my cavern. Also you are to recapture my Magic Belt and return it to me. Will you do this, General Crinkle?"

"No, your Majesty," replied the Nome; "for it can't be done."

"Oh, indeed!" exclaimed the King. Then he

turned to his servants and said: "Please take General Crinkle to the torture chamber. There you will kindly slice him into thin slices. Afterward you may feed him to the seven-headed dogs."

"Anything to oblige your Majesty," replied the servants, politely, and led the condemned man away.

When they had gone the King addressed the army again.

"Listen!" said he. "The General who is to command my armies must promise to carry out my orders. If he fails he will share the fate of poor Crinkle. Now, then, who will volunteer to lead my hosts to the Emerald City?"

For a time no one moved and all were silent. Then an old Nome with white whiskers so long that they were tied around his waist to prevent their tripping him up, stepped out of the ranks and saluted the King.

"I'd like to ask a few questions, your Majesty," he said.

"Go ahead," replied the King.

"These Oz people are quite good, are they not?"

"As good as apple pie," said the King.

"And they are happy, I suppose?" continued the old Nome.

"Happy as the day is long," said the King.

"And contented and prosperous?" inquired the Nome.

"Very much so," said the King.

"Well, your Majesty," remarked he of the white whiskers, "I think I should like to undertake the job, so I'll be your General. I hate good people; I detest happy people; I'm opposed to any one who is contented and prosperous. That is why I am so fond of your Majesty. Make me

your General and I'll promise to conquer and destroy the Oz people. If I fail I'm ready to be sliced thin and fed to the seven-headed dogs."

"Very good! Very good, indeed! That's the way to talk!" cried Roquat the Red, who was greatly pleased. "What is your name, General?"

"I'm called Guph, your Majesty."

"Well, Guph, come with me to my private

cave and we'll talk it over." Then he turned to the army. "Nomes and soldiers," said he, "you are to obey the commands of General Guph until he becomes dog-feed. Any man who fails to obey his new General will be promptly thrown away. You are now dismissed."

Guph went to the King's private cave and sat down upon an amethyst chair and put his feet on the arm of the King's ruby throne. Then he lighted his pipe and threw the live coal he had taken from his pocket upon the King's left foot and puffed the smoke into the King's eyes and made himself comfortable. For he was a wise old Nome, and he knew that the best way to get along with Roquat the Red was to show that he was not afraid of him.

"I'm ready for the talk, your Majesty," he said.

The King coughed and looked at his new General fiercely.

"Do you not tremble to take such liberties with your monarch?" he asked.

"Oh, no," said Guph, calmly, and he blew a wreath of smoke that curled around the King's nose and made him sneeze. "You want to conquer the Emerald City, and I'm the only Nome in your dominions who can conquer it. So you will be very careful not to hurt me until I have carried out your wishes. After that—"

"Well, what then?" inquired the King.

"Then you will be so grateful to me that you won't care to hurt me," replied the General.

"That is a very good argument," said Roquat. "But suppose you fail?"

"Then it's the slicing machine. I agree to that," announced Guph. "But if you do as I tell you there will be no failure. The trouble with

you, Roquat, is that you don't think carefully enough. I do. You would go ahead and march through your tunnel into Oz, and get defeated and driven back. I won't. And the reason I won't is because when I march I'll have all my plans made, and a host of allies to assist my Nomes."

"What do you mean by that?" asked the King.

"I'll explain, King Roquat. You're going to attack a fair country, and a mighty fairy country, too. They haven't much of an army in Oz, but the Princess who rules them has a fairy wand; and the little girl Dorothy has your Magic Belt; and at the North of the Emerald City lives a clever sorceress called Glinda the Good, who commands the spirits of the air. Also I have heard that there is a wonderful Wizard in Ozma's palace, who is so skillful that people used to pay him money in America to see him perform. So you see it will be no easy thing to overcome all this magic."

"We have fifty thousand soldiers!" cried the King, proudly.

"Yes; but they are Nomes," remarked Guph, taking a silk handkerchief from the King's pocket and wiping his own pointed shoes with it. "Nomes are immortals, but they are not strong on magic. When you lost your famous Belt the greater part of your own power was gone from you. Against Ozma you and your Nomes would have no show at all."

Roquat's eyes flashed angrily.

"Then away you go to the slicing machine!" he cried.

"Not yet," said the General, filling his pipe

from the King's private tobacco pouch.

"What do you propose to do?" asked the monarch.

"I propose to obtain the power we need," answered Guph. "There are a good many evil creatures who have magic powers sufficient to destroy and conquer the Land of Oz. We will get them on our side, band them all together, and then take Ozma and her people by surprise. It's all very simple and easy when you know how. Alone we should be helpless to injure the Ruler of Oz, but with the aid of the evil powers we can summon we shall easily succeed."

King Roquat was delighted with this idea, for he realized how clever it was.

"Surely, Guph, you are the greatest General I have ever had!" he exclaimed, his eyes sparkling with joy. "You must go at once and make arrangements with the evil powers to assist us,

39

and meantime I'll begin to dig the tunnel."

"I thought you'd agree with me, Roquat," replied the new General. "I'll start this very afternoon to visit the Chief of the Whimsies."

How DOROTHY BECAME A PRINCESS

CHAPTER FIVE

WHEN the people of the Emerald City heard that Dorothy had returned to them every one was eager to see her, for the little girl was a general favorite in the Land of Oz. From time to time some of the folk from the great outside world had found their way into this fairyland, but all except one had been companions of Dorothy and had turned out to be very agreeable people. The exception I speak of was the wonderful Wizard of Oz, a sleight-of-hand performer from Omaha who went up in a balloon and was carried by a current of air to the Emerald City. His queer and puzzling tricks made the people of Oz believe him a great wizard for a time, and he ruled over them until Dorothy arrived on her first visit and showed the Wizard to be a mere humbug. He was a gentle, kindly-hearted little man, and Dorothy grew to like him afterward. When, after an absence, the Wizard returned to the Land of Oz, Ozma received him graciously and gave him a home in a part of the palace.

In addition to the Wizard two other personages from the outside world had been allowed to make their home in the Emerald City. The first was a quaint Shaggy Man, whom Ozma had made the Governor of the Royal Storehouses, and the second a Yellow Hen named Billina, who had a fine house in the gardens back of the palace, where she looked after a large family. Both these had been old comrades of Dorothy, so you see the little girl was quite an important personage in Oz, and the people thought she had brought them good luck, and loved her next best to Ozma. During her several visits this little girl had been the means of destroying two wicked witches who oppressed the people, and she had discovered a live scarecrow who was now one of the most popular personages in all the fairy country. With the Scarecrow's help she had rescued Nick Chopper, a Tin Woodman, who had rusted in a lonely forest, and the tin man was now the Emperor of the Country of the Winkies and much beloved because of his kind heart. No wonder the people thought Dorothy had brought them good luck! Yet, strange as it may seem, she had accomplished all these wonders not because she was a fairy or had any magical powers whatever, but because she was a simple, sweet and true little girl who was honest to herself and to all whom she met. In this world in which we live simplicity and kindness are the only magic wands that work wonders, and in the Land of Oz Dorothy found these same qualities had won for her the love and admiration of the people. Indeed, the little girl had made many warm friends in the fairy country, and the only real grief the Ozites had ever experienced was when Dorothy left them and returned to her Kansas home.

Now she received a joyful welcome, although no one except Ozma knew at first that she had finally come to stay for good and all.

That evening Dorothy had many callers, and among them were such important people as Tiktok, a machine man who thought and spoke and moved by clockwork; her old companion the genial Shaggy Man; Jack Pumpkinhead, whose body was brush-wood and whose head was a ripe pumpkin with a face carved upon it; the Cowardly Lion and the Hungry Tiger, two great beasts from the forest, who served Princess Ozma, and Professor H. M. Wogglebug, T. E. This wogglebug was a remarkable creature. He had once been a tiny little bug, crawling around in a school-room, but he was discovered and highly magnified so that he could be seen more plainly, and while in this magnified condition he had escaped. He had always remained big, and he dressed like a dandy and was so full of knowledge and information (which are distinct acquirements), that he had been made a Professor and the head of the Royal College.

Dorothy had a nice visit with these old friends, and also talked a long time with the Wizard, who was little and old and withered and dried up, but as merry and active as a child. Afterward she went to see Billina's fast growing family of chicks.

Toto, Dorothy's little black dog, also met with a cordial reception. Toto was an especial friend of the Shaggy Man, and he knew every one else. Being the only dog in the Land of Oz, he was highly respected by the people, who believed animals entitled to every consideration if they behaved themselves properly.

Dorothy had four lovely rooms in the palace, which were always reserved for her use and were called "Dorothy's rooms." These consisted of a beautiful sitting room, a dressing room, a dainty bedchamber and a big marble bathroom. And in these rooms were everything that heart could desire, placed there with loving thoughtfulness by Ozma for her little friend's use. The royal dressmakers had the little girl's measure, so they kept the closets in her dressing room filled with lovely dresses of every description and suitable for every occasion. No wonder Dorothy had refrained from bringing with her her old calico and gingham dresses! Here everything that was dear to a little girl's heart was supplied in profusion, and nothing so rich and beautiful could ever have been found in the biggest department stores in America. Of course Dorothy enjoyed all these luxuries, and the only reason she had heretofore preferred to live in Kansas was because her uncle and aunt loved her and needed her with them.

Now, however, all was to be changed, and Dorothy was really more delighted to know that her dear relatives were to share in her good fortune and enjoy the delights of the Land of Oz, than she was to possess such luxury for herself.

Next morning, at Ozma's request, Dorothy dressed herself in a pretty sky-blue gown of rich silk, trimmed with real pearls. The buckles of her shoes were set with pearls, too, and more of these priceless gems were on a lovely coronet which she wore upon her forehead.

"For," said her friend Ozma, "from this time forth, my dear, you must assume your rightful rank as a Princess of Oz, and being my chosen companion you must dress in a way befitting the dignity of your position."

Dorothy agreed to this, although she knew that neither gowns nor jewels could make her anything else than the simple, unaffected little girl she had always been.

As soon as they had breakfasted—the girls eating together in Ozma's pretty boudoir—the Ruler of Oz said:

"Now, dear friend, we will use the Magic Belt to transport your uncle and aunt from Kansas to the Emerald City. But I think it would be fitting, in receiving such distinguished guests, for us to sit in my Throne Room."

"Oh, they're not very 'stinguished, Ozma," said Dorothy. "They're just plain people, like me."

"Being your friends and relatives, Princess Dorothy, they are certainly distinguished," replied the Ruler, with a smile.

"They—they won't hardly know what to make of all your splendid furniture and things," protested Dorothy, gravely. "It may scare 'em to see your grand Throne Room, an' p'raps we'd better go into the back yard, Ozma, where the cabbages grow an' the chickens are playing. Then it would seem more natural to Uncle Henry and Aunt Em."

"No; they shall first see me in my Throne Room," replied Ozma, decidedly; and when she spoke in that tone Dorothy knew it was not wise to oppose her, for Ozma was accustomed to having her own way.

So together they went to the Throne Room, an immense domed chamber in the center of the palace. Here stood the royal throne, made of solid gold and encrusted with enough precious stones to stock a dozen jewelry stores in our country.

Ozma, who was wearing the Magic Belt, seated herself in the throne, and Dorothy sat at her feet. In the room were assembled many ladies and gentlemen of the court, clothed in rich apparel and wearing fine jewelry. Two immense animals squatted, one on each side of the throne—the Cowardly Lion and the Hungry Tiger. In a balcony high up in the dome an orchestra played sweet music, and beneath the dome two electric fountains sent sprays of colored perfumed water shooting up nearly as high as the arched ceiling.

"Are you ready, Dorothy?" asked the Ruler.

"I am," replied Dorothy; "but I don't know whether Aunt Em and Uncle Henry are ready."

"That won't matter," declared Ozma. "The old life can have very little to interest them, and the sooner they begin the new life here the happier they will be. Here they come, my dear!"

As she spoke, there before the throne appeared Uncle Henry and Aunt Em, who for a moment stood motionless, glaring with white and startled faces at the scene that confronted them. If the ladies and gentlemen present had not been so polite I am sure they would have laughed at the two strangers.

Aunt Em had her calico dress skirt "tucked up," and she wore a faded blue-checked apron. Her hair was rather straggly and she had on a pair of Uncle Henry's old slippers. In one hand she held a dish-towel and in the other a cracked earthenware plate, which she had been engaged in wiping when so suddenly transported to the Land of Oz.

Uncle Henry, when the summons came, had been out in the barn "doin' chores." He wore a ragged and much soiled straw hat, a checked shirt without any collar and blue overalls tucked into the tops of his old cowhide boots.

"By gum!" gasped Uncle Henry, looking around as if bewildered.

"Well, I swan!" gurgled Aunt Em, in a hoarse, frightened voice. Then her eyes fell upon Dorothy, and she said: "D-d-d-don't that look like our little girl—our Dorothy, Henry?"

"Hi, there—look out, Em!" exclaimed the old man, as Aunt Em advanced a step; "take care o' the wild beastses, or you're a goner!"

But now Dorothy sprang forward and embraced and kissed her aunt and uncle affectionately, afterward taking their hands in her own.

"Don't be afraid," she said to them. "You are now in the Land of Oz, where you are to live always, and be comfer'ble an' happy. You'll never have to worry over anything again, 'cause there won't be anything to worry about. And you owe it all to the kindness of my friend Princess Ozma."

Here she led them before the throne and continued:

"Your Highness, this is Uncle Henry. And this is Aunt Em. They want to thank you for bringing them here from Kansas."

Aunt Em tried to "slick" her hair, and she hid the dishtowel and dish under her apron while she bowed to the lovely Ozma. Uncle Henry took off his straw hat and held it awkwardly in his hands.

But the Ruler of Oz rose and came from her throne to greet her newly arrived guests, and she smiled as sweetly upon them as if they had been a king and a queen.

"You are very welcome here, where I have brought you for Princess Dorothy's sake," she said, graciously, "and I hope you will be quite happy in your new home." Then she turned to her courtiers, who were silently and gravely regarding the scene, and added: "I present to my people our Princess Dorothy's beloved Uncle Henry and Aunt Em, who will hereafter be subjects of our kingdom. It will please me to have you show them every kindness and honor in your power, and to join me in making them happy and contented."

Hearing this, all those assembled bowed low and respectfully to the old farmer and his wife, who bobbed their own heads in return.

"And now," said Ozma to them, "Dorothy will show you the rooms prepared for you. I hope you will like them, and shall expect you to join me at luncheon."

So Dorothy led her relatives away, and as soon as they were out of the Throne Room and alone in the corridor Aunt Em squeezed Dorothy's hand and said:

"Child, child! How in the world did we ever get here so quick? And is it all real? And are we to stay here, as she says? And what does it all mean, anyhow?"

Dorothy laughed.

"Why didn't you tell us what you were goin' to do?" inquired Uncle Henry, reproachfully. "If I'd known about it I'd 'a put on my Sunday clothes."

"I'll 'splain ever'thing as soon as we get to your rooms," promised Dorothy. "You're in great luck, Uncle Henry and Aunt Em; an' so am I! And oh! I'm so happy to have got you here, at last!"

As he walked by the little girl's side Uncle Henry stroked his whiskers thoughtfully.

" 'Pears to me, Dorothy, we won't make

51

bang-up fairies," he remarked.

"An' my back hair looks like a fright!" wailed Aunt Em.

"Never mind," returned the little girl, reassuringly. "You won't have anything to do now but to look pretty, Aunt Em; an' Uncle Henry won't have to work till his back aches, that's certain."

"Sure?" they asked, wonderingly, and in the same breath.

"Course I'm sure," said Dorothy. "You're in the Fairyland of Oz, now; an' what's more, you belong to it!"

How GUPH VISITED THE WHIMSIES

CHAPTER SIX

THE new General of the Nome King's army knew perfectly well that to fail in his plans meant death for him. Yet he was not at all anxious or worried. He hated every one who was good and longed to make all who were happy unhappy. Therefore he had accepted this dangerous position as General quite willingly, feeling sure in his evil mind that he would be able to do a lot of mischief and finally conquer the Land of Oz.

Yet Guph determined to be careful, and to lay his plans well, so as not to fail. He argued that only careless people fail in what they attempt to do.

The mountains underneath which the Nome King's extensive caverns were located lay grouped just north of the Land of Ev, which lay directly across the deadly desert to the east of the Land of Oz. As the mountains were also on the edge of the desert the Nome King found that he had only to tunnel underneath the desert to reach Ozma's dominions. He did not wish his armies to appear above ground in the Country of the Winkies, which was the part of the Land of Oz nearest to King Roquat's own country, as then the people would give the alarm and enable Ozma to fortify the Emerald City and assemble an army. He wanted to take all the Oz people by surprise; so he decided to run the tunnel clear through to the Emerald City, where he and his hosts could break through the ground without warning and conquer the people before they had time to defend themselves.

Roquat the Red began work at once upon his tunnel, setting a thousand miners at the task and building it high and broad enough for his armies to march through it with ease. The Nomes were used to making tunnels, as all the kingdom in which they lived was under ground; so they made rapid progress.

While this work was going on General Guph started out alone to visit the Chief of the Whimsies.

These Whimsies were curious people who lived in a retired country of their own. They had large, strong bodies, but heads so small that they were no bigger than door-knobs. Of course, such tiny heads could not contain any great amount of brains, and the Whimsies were so ashamed of their personal appearance and lack of commonsense that they wore big heads, made of pasteboard, which they fastened over their own little heads. On these pasteboard heads they sewed sheep's wool for hair, and the wool was colored many tints—pink, green and lavender being the favorite colors.

The faces of these false heads were painted in many ridiculous ways, according to the whims of the owners, and these big, burly creatures looked so whimsical and absurd in their queer masks that they were called "Whimsies." They foolishly imagined that no one would suspect the little heads that were inside the imitation ones, not knowing that it is folly to try to appear otherwise than as nature has made us.

The Chief of the Whimsies had as little wisdom as the others, and had been chosen chief merely because none among them was any wiser or more capable of ruling. The Whimsies were evil spirits and could not be killed. They were hated and feared by every one and were known as terrible fighters because they were so strong and muscular and had not sense enough to know when they were defeated.

General Guph thought the Whimsies would be a great help to the Nomes in the conquest of

Oz, for under his leadership they could be induced to fight as long as they could stand up. So he traveled to their country and asked to see the Chief, who lived in a house that had a picture of his grotesque false head painted over the doorway.

The Chief's false head had blue hair, a turned-up nose, and a mouth that stretched half across the face. Big green eyes had been painted upon it, but in the center of the chin were two small holes made in the pasteboard, so that the Chief could see through them with his own tiny eyes; for when the big head was fastened upon his shoulders the eyes in his own natural head were on a level with the false chin.

Said General Guph to the Chief of the Whimsies:

"We Nomes are going to conquer the Land of Oz and capture our King's Magic Belt, which the Oz people stole from him. Then we are going to plunder and destroy the whole country. And we want the Whimsies to help us."

"Will there be any fighting?" asked the Chief.

"Plenty," replied Guph.

That must have pleased the Chief, for he got up and danced around the room three times. Then he seated himself again, adjusted his false head, and said:

"We have no quarrel with Ozma of Oz."

"But you Whimsies love to fight, and here is a splendid chance to do so," urged Guph.

"Wait till I sing a song," said the Chief. Then he lay back in his chair and sang a foolish song that did not seem to the General to mean anything, although he listened carefully. When he had finished, the Chief Whimsie looked at him through the holes in his chin and asked:

"What reward will you give us if we help you?"

The General was prepared for this question, for he had been thinking the matter over on his journey. People often do a good deed without hope of reward, but for an evil deed they always demand payment.

"When we get our Magic Belt," he made reply, "our King, Roquat the Red, will use its power to give every Whimsie a natural head as big and fine as the false head he now wears. Then you will no longer be ashamed because your big strong bodies have such teeny-weenty heads."

"Oh! Will you do that?" asked the Chief, eagerly.

"We surely will," promised the General.

"I'll talk to my people," said the Chief.

So he called a meeting of all the Whimsies and told them of the offer made by the Nomes. The creatures were delighted with the bargain, and at once agreed to fight for the Nome King and help him to conquer Oz.

One Whimsie alone seemed to have a glimmer of sense, for he asked:

"Suppose we fail to capture the Magic Belt? What will happen then, and what good will all our fighting do?"

But they threw him into the river for asking foolish questions, and laughed when the water ruined his pasteboard head before he could swim out again.

So the compact was made and General Guph was delighted with his success in gaining such powerful allies.

But there were other people, too, just as important as the Whimsies, whom the clever old Nome had determined to win to his side.

How AUNT EM CONQUERED THE LION

CHAPTER SEVEN

"THESE are your rooms," said Dorothy, opening a door.

Aunt Em drew back at sight of the splendid furniture and draperies.

"Ain't there any place to wipe my feet?" she asked.

"You will soon change your slippers for new shoes," replied Dorothy. "Don't be afraid, Aunt Em. Here is where you are to live, so walk right in and make yourself at home."

Aunt Em advanced hesitatingly.

"It beats the Topeka Hotel!" she cried, admiringly. "But this place is too grand for us, child. Can't we have some back room in the attic, that's more in our class?"

"No," said Dorothy. "You've got to live here, 'cause Ozma says so. And all the rooms in this palace are just as fine as these, and some are better. It won't do any good to fuss, Aunt Em. You've got to be swell and high-toned in the Land of Oz, whether you want to or not; so you may as well make up your mind to it."

"It's hard luck," replied her aunt, looking around with an awed expression; "but folks can get used to anything, if they try. Eh, Henry?"

"Why, as to that," said Uncle Henry, slowly, "I b'lieve in takin' what's pervided us, an' askin' no questions. I've traveled some, Em, in my time, and you hain't; an' that makes a difference atween us."

Then Dorothy showed them through the rooms. The first was a handsome sitting-room, with windows opening upon the rose gardens. Then came separate bedrooms for Aunt Em and Uncle Henry, with a fine bathroom between them. Aunt Em had a pretty dressing room, besides, and Dorothy opened the closets and showed several exquisite costumes that had been provided for her aunt by the royal dressmakers, who had worked all night to get them ready. Everything that Aunt Em could possibly need was in the drawers and closets, and her dressing-table was covered with engraved gold toilet articles.

Uncle Henry had nine suits of clothes, cut in the popular Munchkin fashion, with knee-breeches, silk stockings and low shoes with

jeweled buckles. The hats to match these costumes had painted tops and wide brims with
small gold bells around the edges. His shirts
were of fine linen with frilled bosoms, and his
vests were richly embroidered with colored silks.

Uncle Henry decided that he would first take
a bath and then dress himself in a blue satin
suit that had caught his fancy. He accepted his
good fortune with calm composure and refused
to have a servant to assist him. But Aunt Em was
"all of a flutter," as she said, and it took Dorothy
and Jellia Jamb, the housekeeper, and two maids
a long time to dress her and do up her hair and
get her "rigged like a popinjay," as she quaintly
expressed it. She wanted to stop and admire
everything that caught her eye, and she sighed
continually and declared that such finery was
too good for an old country woman, and that
she never thought she would have to "put on
airs" at her time of life.

Finally she was dressed, and when they went
into the sitting-room there was Uncle Henry in
his blue satin, walking gravely up and down the
room. He had trimmed his beard and mustache
and looked very dignified and respectable.

"Tell me, Dorothy," he said; "do all the men
here wear duds like these?"

"Yes," she replied; "all 'cept the Scarecrow
and the Shaggy Man—and of course the Tin

Woodman and Tiktok, who are made of metal. You'll find all the men at Ozma's court dressed just as you are—only perhaps a little finer."

"Henry, you look like a play-actor," announced Aunt Em, looking at her husband critically.

"An' you, Em, look more highfalutin' than a peacock," he replied.

"I guess you're right," she said, regretfully; "but we're helpless victims of high-toned royalty."

Dorothy was much amused.

"Come with me," she said, "and I'll show you 'round the palace."

She took them through the beautiful rooms and introduced them to all the people they chanced to meet. Also she showed them her own pretty rooms, which were not far from their own.

"So it's all true," said Aunt Em, wide-eyed with amazement, "and what Dorothy told us of this fairy country was plain facts instead of dreams! But where are all the strange creatures you used to know here?"

"Yes; where's the Scarecrow?" inquired Uncle Henry.

"Why, he's just now away on a visit to the Tin Woodman, who is Emp'ror of the Winkie Country," answered the little girl. "You'll see him when he comes back, and you're sure to like him."

"And where's the Wonderful Wizard?" asked Aunt Em.

"You'll see him at Ozma's luncheon, for he lives in this palace," was the reply.

"And Jack Pumpkinhead?"

"Oh, he lives a little way out of town, in his own pumpkin field. We'll go there some time and see him, and we'll call on Professor Wogglebug, too. The Shaggy Man will be at the luncheon, I guess, and Tiktok. And now I'll take you out to see Billina, who has a house of her own."

So they went into the back yard, and after walking along winding paths some distance through the beautiful gardens they came to an attractive little house where the Yellow Hen sat on the front porch sunning herself.

"Good morning, my dear Mistress," called Billina, fluttering down to meet them. "I was expecting you to call, for I heard you had come back and brought your uncle and aunt with you."

"We're here for good and all, this time, Billina," cried Dorothy, joyfully. "Uncle Henry and Aunt Em belong in Oz now as much as I do!"

"Then they are very lucky people," declared Billina; "for there couldn't be a nicer place to live. But come, my dear; I must show you all my Dorothys. Nine are living and have grown up to be very respectable hens; but one took cold at Ozma's birthday party and died of the pip, and the other two turned out to be horrid roosters, so I had to change their names from Dorothy to Daniel. They all had the letter 'D' engraved upon their gold lockets, you remember, with your picture inside, and 'D' stands for Daniel as well as for Dorothy."

"Did you call both the roosters Daniel?" asked Uncle Henry.

"Yes, indeed. I've nine Dorothys and two Daniels; and the nine Dorothys have eighty-six sons and daughters and over three hundred grandchildren," said Billina, proudly.

"What names do you give 'em all, dear?" inquired the little girl.

"Oh, they are all Dorothys and Daniels, some being Juniors and some Double-Juniors. Dorothy and Daniel are two good names, and I see no object in hunting for others," declared the Yellow Hen. "But just think, Dorothy, what a big chicken family we've grown to be, and our numbers increase nearly every day! Ozma doesn't know what to do with all the eggs we lay, and we are never eaten or harmed in any way, as chickens are in your country. They give us everything to make us contented and happy, and I, my dear, am the acknowledged Queen and Governor of every chicken in Oz, because I'm the eldest and started the whole colony."

"You ought to be very proud, ma'am," said Uncle Henry, who was astonished to hear a hen talk so sensibly.

"Oh, I am," she replied. "I've the loveliest pearl necklace you ever saw. Come in the house and I'll show it to you. And I've nine leg bracelets and a diamond pin for each wing. But I only wear them on state occasions."

They followed the Yellow Hen into the house, which Aunt Em declared was neat as a pin. They could not sit down, because all Billina's chairs were roosting-poles made of silver;

so they had to stand while the hen fussily showed them her treasures.

Then they had to go into the back rooms occupied by Billina's nine Dorothys and two Daniels, who were all plump yellow chickens and greeted the visitors very politely. It was easy to see that they were well bred and that Billina had looked after their education.

In the yards were all the children and grandchildren of these eleven elders and they were of all sizes, from well-grown hens to tiny chickens just out of the shell. About fifty fluffy yellow youngsters were at school, being taught good manners and good grammar by a young hen who wore spectacles. They sang in chorus a patriotic song of the Land of Oz, in honor of their visitors, and Aunt Em was much impressed by these talking chickens.

Dorothy wanted to stay and play with the young chickens for a while, but Uncle Henry and Aunt Em had not seen the palace grounds and gardens yet and were eager to get better acquainted with the marvelous and delightful land in which they were to live.

"I'll stay here, and you can go for a walk," said Dorothy. "You'll be perfec'ly safe anywhere, and may do whatever you want to. When you get tired, go back to the palace and find your rooms, and I'll come to you before luncheon is ready."

So Uncle Henry and Aunt Em started out alone to explore the grounds, and Dorothy knew that they couldn't get lost, because all the palace grounds were enclosed by a high wall of green marble set with emeralds.

It was a rare treat to these simple folk, who had lived in the country all their lives and known little enjoyment of any sort, to wear beautiful clothes and live in a palace and be treated with respect and consideration by all around them. They were very happy indeed as they strolled up the shady walks and looked upon the gorgeous flowers and shrubs, feeling that their new home was more beautiful than any tongue could describe.

Suddenly, as they turned a corner and walked through a gap in a high hedge, they came face to face with an enormous Lion, which crouched upon the green lawn and seemed surprised by their appearance.

They stopped short, Uncle Henry trembling with horror and Aunt Em too terrified to scream. Next moment the poor woman clasped her husband around the neck and cried:

"Save me, Henry, save me!"

"Can't even save myself, Em," he returned, in a husky voice, "for the animile looks as if it could eat both of us, an' lick its chops for more! If I only had a gun—"

"Haven't you, Henry? Haven't you?" she asked anxiously.

"Nary gun, Em. So let's die as brave an' graceful as we can. I knew our luck couldn't last!"

"I won't die. I won't be eaten by a lion!" wailed Aunt Em, glaring upon the huge beast. Then a thought struck her, and she whispered: "Henry, I've heard as savage beastses can be conquered by the human eye. I'll eye that lion out o' countenance an' save our lives."

"Try it, Em," he returned, also in a whisper. "Look at him as you do at me when I'm late to dinner."

Aunt Em turned upon the Lion a determined countenance and a wild dilated eye. She glared at the immense beast steadily, and the Lion, who had been quietly blinking at them, began to appear uneasy and disturbed.

"Is anything the matter, ma'am?" he asked, in a mild voice.

At this speech from the terrible beast Aunt Em and Uncle Henry both were startled, and then Uncle Henry remembered that this must be the Lion they had seen in Ozma's Throne Room.

"Hold on, Em!" he exclaimed. "Quit the eagle

eye conquest an' take courage. I guess this is the same Cowardly Lion Dorothy has told us about."

"Oh, is it?" she asked, much relieved.

"When he spoke, I got the idea; and when he looked so 'shamed like, I was sure of it," Uncle Henry continued.

Aunt Em regarded the animal with new interest.

"Are you the Cowardly Lion?" she inquired. "Are you Dorothy's friend?"

"Yes'm," answered the Lion, meekly. "Dorothy and I are old chums and are very fond of each other. I'm the King of Beasts, you know, and the Hungry Tiger and I serve Princess Ozma as her body guards."

"To be sure," said Aunt Em, nodding. "But the King of Beasts shouldn't be cowardly."

"I've heard that said before," remarked the Lion, yawning till he showed his two great rows of sharp white teeth; "but that does not keep me from being frightened whenever I go into battle."

"What do you do, run?" asked Uncle Henry.

"No; that would be foolish, for the enemy would run after me," declared the Lion. "So I tremble with fear and pitch in as hard as I can; and so far I have always won my fight."

"Ah, I begin to understand," said Uncle Henry.

"Were you scared when I looked at you just now?" inquired Aunt Em.

"Terribly scared, madam," answered the Lion, "for at first I thought you were going to have a fit. Then I noticed you were trying to overcome me by the power of your eye, and your glance was so fierce and penetrating that I shook with fear."

This greatly pleased the lady, and she said quite cheerfully:

"Well, I won't hurt you, so don't be scared any more. I just wanted to see what the human eye was good for."

"The human eye is a fearful weapon," remarked the Lion, scratching his nose softly with his paw to hide a smile. "Had I not known you were Dorothy's friends I might have torn you

both into shreds in order to escape your terrible gaze."

Aunt Em shuddered at hearing this, and Uncle Henry said hastily:

"I'm glad you knew us. Good morning, Mr. Lion; we'll hope to see you again—by and by—some time in the future."

"Good morning," replied the Lion, squatting down upon the lawn again. "You are likely to see a good deal of me, if you live in the Land of Oz."

How THE GRAND GALLIPOOT JOINED THE NOMES

CHAPTER EIGHT

AFTER leaving the Whimsies, Guph continued on his journey and penetrated far into the Northwest. He wanted to get to the Country of the Growleywogs, and in order to do that he must cross the Ripple Land, which was a hard thing to do. For the Ripple Land was a succession of hills and valleys, all very steep and rocky, and they changed places constantly by rippling. While Guph was climbing a hill it sank down under him and became a valley, and while he was descending into a valley it rose up and carried him to the top of a hill. This was very perplexing to the traveler, and a stranger might have thought he could never cross the Ripple Land at all. But Guph knew that if he kept steadily on he would get to the end at last; so he paid no attention to the changing hills and valleys and plodded along as calmly as if walking upon the level ground.

The result of this wise persistence was that the General finally reached firmer soil and, after penetrating a dense forest, came to the Dominion of the Growleywogs.

No sooner had he crossed the border of this domain when two guards seized him and carried him before the Grand Gallipoot of the Growleywogs, who scowled upon him ferociously and asked him why he dared intrude upon his territory.

"I'm the Lord High General of the Invincible Army of the Nomes, and my name is Guph," was the reply. "All the world trembles when that name is mentioned."

The Growleywogs gave a shout of jeering laughter at this, and one of them caught the Nome in his strong arms and tossed him high into the air. Guph was considerably shaken when he fell upon the hard ground, but he appeared to take no notice of the impertinence and composed himself to speak again to the Grand Gallipoot.

"My master, King Roquat the Red, has sent me here to confer with you. He wishes your assistance to conquer the Land of Oz."

Here the General paused, and the Grand Gallipoot scowled upon him more terribly than ever and said:

"Go on!"

The voice of the Grand Gallipoot was partly a roar and partly a growl. He mumbled his words badly and Guph had to listen carefully in order to understand him.

These Growleywogs were certainly remarkable creatures. They were of gigantic size, yet were all bone and skin and muscle, there being no meat or fat upon their bodies at all. Their powerful muscles lay just underneath their skins, like bunches of tough rope, and the weakest Growleywog was so strong that he could pick up an elephant and toss it seven miles away.

It seems unfortunate that strong people are usually so disagreeable and overbearing that no one cares for them. In fact, to be different from your fellow creatures is always a misfortune. The Growleywogs knew that they were disliked and avoided by every one, so they had become surly and unsociable even among themselves. Guph knew that they hated all people, including the Nomes; but he hoped to win them over, nevertheless, and knew that if he succeeded they would afford him very powerful assistance.

"The Land of Oz is ruled by a namby-pamby girl who is disgustingly kind and good," he continued. "Her people are all happy and contented and have no care or worries whatever."

"Go on!" growled the Grand Gallipoot.

"Once the Nome King enslaved the Royal Family of Ev—another goody-goody lot that we detest," said the General. "But Ozma interfered, although it was none of her business, and marched her army against us. With her was a Kansas girl named Dorothy, and a Yellow Hen, and they marched directly into the Nome King's cavern. There they liberated our slaves from Ev and stole King Roquat's Magic Belt, which they carried away with them. So now our King is making a tunnel under the deadly desert, so we can march through it to the Emerald City. When we get there we mean to conquer and destroy all the land and recapture the Magic Belt."

Again he paused, and again the Grand Gallipoot growled:

"Go on!"

Guph tried to think what to say next, and a happy thought soon occurred to him.

"We want you to help us in this conquest," he announced, "for we need the mighty aid of the Growleywogs in order to make sure that we shall not be defeated. You are the strongest people in all the world, and you hate good and happy creatures as much as we Nomes do. I am sure it will be a real pleasure to you to tear down the beautiful Emerald City, and in return for your valuable assistance we will allow you to bring back to your country ten thousand people of Oz, to be your slaves."

"Twenty thousand!" growled the Grand Gallipoot.

"All right, we promise you twenty thousand," agreed the General.

The Gallipoot made a signal and at once his attendants picked up General Guph and carried him away to a prison, where the jailor amused himself by sticking pins in the round fat body of the old Nome, to see him jump and hear him yell.

But while this was going on the Grand Gallipoot was talking with his counselors, who were the most important officials of the Growleywogs. When he had stated to them the proposition of the Nome King he said:

"My advice is to offer to help them. Then, when we have conquered the Land of Oz, we will take not only our twenty thousand prisoners but all the gold and jewels we want."

"Let us take the Magic Belt, too," suggested one counselor.

"And rob the Nome King and make him our slave," said another.

"That is a good idea," declared the Grand Gallipoot. "I'd like King Roquat for my own slave. He could black my boots and bring me my porridge every morning while I am in bed."

"There is a famous Scarecrow in Oz. I'll take him for my slave," said a counselor.

"I'll take Tiktok, the machine man," said another.

"Give me the Tin Woodman," said a third.

They went on for some time, dividing up the people and the treasure of Oz in advance of the conquest. For they had no doubt at all that they would be able to destroy Ozma's domain. Were they not the strongest people in all the world?

"The deadly desert has kept us out of Oz before," remarked the Grand Gallipoot, "but now that the Nome King is building a tunnel we shall get into the Emerald City very easily. So let us send the little fat General back to his King with our promise to assist him. We will not say that we intend to conquer the Nomes after we have conquered Oz, but we will do so, just the same."

This plan being agreed upon, they all went home to dinner, leaving General Guph still in prison. The Nome had no idea that he had succeeded in his mission, for finding himself in prison he feared the Growleywogs intended to put him to death.

By this time the jailor had tired of sticking pins in the General, and was amusing himself by carefully pulling the Nome's whiskers out by the roots, one at a time. This enjoyment was interrupted by the Grand Gallipoot sending for the prisoner.

"Wait a few hours," begged the jailor. "I haven't pulled out a quarter of his whiskers yet."

"If you keep the Grand Gallipoot waiting he'll break your back," declared the messenger.

"Perhaps you're right," sighed the jailor.

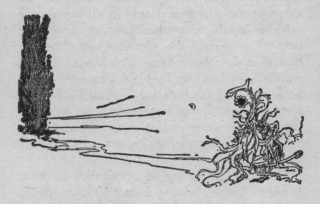

"Take the prisoner away, if you will, but I advise you to kick him at every step he takes. It will be good fun, for he is as soft as a ripe peach."

So Guph was led away to the royal castle, where the Grand Gallipoot told him that the Growleywogs had decided to assist the Nomes in conquering the Land of Oz.

"Whenever you are ready," he added, "send me word and I will march with eighteen thousand of my most powerful warriors to your aid."

Guph was so delighted that he forgot all the smarting caused by the pins and the pulling of whiskers. He did not even complain of the treatment he had received, but thanked the Grand Gallipoot and hurried away upon his journey.

He had now secured the assistance of the Whimsies and the Growleywogs; but his success made him long for still more allies. His own life depended upon his conquering Oz, and he said to himself:

"I'll take no chances. I'll be certain of success. Then, when Oz is destroyed, perhaps I shall be a greater man than old Roquat, and I can throw him away and be King of the Nomes myself. Why not? The Whimsies are stronger than the Nomes, and they are my friends. The Growleywogs are stronger than the Whimsies, and they also are my friends. There are some people still stronger than the Growleywogs, and if I can but induce them to aid me I shall have nothing more to fear."

How THE WOGGLEBUG TAUGHT ATHLETICS

CHAPTER NINE

IT did not take Dorothy long to establish herself in her new home, for she knew the people and the manners and customs of the Emerald City just as well as she knew the old Kansas farm.

But Uncle Henry and Aunt Em had some trouble in getting used to the finery and pomp and ceremony of Ozma's palace, and felt uneasy because they were obliged to be "dressed up" all the time. Yet every one was very courteous and kind to them and endeavored to make them happy. Ozma, especially, made much of Dorothy's relatives, for her little friend's sake, and she well knew that the awkwardness and strangeness of their new mode of life would all wear off in time.

The old people were chiefly troubled by the fact that there was no work for them to do.

"Ev'ry day is like Sunday, now," declared Aunt Em, solemnly, "and I can't say I like it. If they'd only let me do up the dishes after meals, or even sweep an' dust my own rooms, I'd be a deal happier. Henry don't know what to do with himself either, and once when he stole out an' fed the chickens Billina scolded him for letting 'em eat between meals. I never knew before what a hardship it is to be rich and have everything you want."

These complaints began to worry Dorothy; so she had a long talk with Ozma upon the subject.

"I see I must find them something to do," said the girlish Ruler of Oz, seriously. "I have been watching your uncle and aunt, and I believe they will be more contented if occupied with some light tasks. While I am considering this matter, Dorothy, you might make a trip with them through the Land of Oz, visiting some of the odd corners and introducing your relatives to some of our curious people."

"Oh, that would be fine!" exclaimed Dorothy, eagerly.

"I will give you an escort befitting your rank as a Princess," continued Ozma; "and you may go to some of the places you have not yet visited yourself, as well as some others that you know. I will mark out a plan of the trip for you and have everything in readiness for you to start to-morrow morning. Take your time, dear, and be gone as long as you wish. By the time you return I shall have found some occupation for Uncle Henry and Aunt Em that will keep them from being restless and dissatisfied."

Dorothy thanked her good friend and kissed the lovely Ruler gratefully. Then she ran to tell the joyful news to her uncle and aunt.

Next morning, after breakfast, everything was found ready for their departure.

The escort included Omby Amby, the Captain General of Ozma's army, which consisted merely of twenty-seven officers besides the Captain General. Once Omby Amby had been a private soldier—the only private in the army—but as there was never any fight to do Ozma saw no need of a private, so she made Omby Amby the highest officer of them all. He was very tall and slim and wore a gay uniform and a fierce mustache. Yet the mustache was the only fierce thing about Omby Amby, whose nature was as gentle as that of a child.

The wonderful Wizard had asked to join the party, and with him came his friend the Shaggy Man, who was shaggy but not ragged, being dressed in fine silks with satin shags and bob-tails. The Shaggy Man had shaggy whiskers and hair, but a sweet disposition and a soft, pleasant voice.

There was an open wagon, with three seats for the passengers, and the wagon was drawn by the famous wooden Sawhorse which had once been brought to life by Ozma by means of a magic powder. The Sawhorse wore golden shoes to keep his wooden legs from wearing away, and he was strong and swift. As this curious creature was Ozma's own favorite steed, and very popular with all the people of the Emerald City, Dorothy knew that she had been highly favored by being permitted to use the Sawhorse on her journey.

In the front seat of the wagon sat Dorothy and the Wizard. Uncle Henry and Aunt Em sat in the next seat and the Shaggy Man and Omby Amby in the third seat. Of course Toto was with the party, curled up at Dorothy's feet, and just as they were about to start Billina came fluttering along the path and begged to be taken with them. Dorothy readily agreed, so the Yellow Hen flew up and perched herself upon the dashboard. She wore her pearl necklace and three bracelets upon each leg, in honor of the occasion.

Dorothy kissed Ozma good-bye, and all the people standing around waved their handkerchiefs, and the band in an upper balcony struck up a military march. Then the Wizard clucked to the Sawhorse and said: "Gid-dap!" and the wooden animal pranced away and drew behind him the big red wagon and all the passengers, without any effort at all. A servant threw open a gate of the palace enclosure, that they might pass out; and so, with music and shouts following them, the journey was begun.

"It's almost like a circus," said Aunt Em, proudly. "I can't help feelin' high an' mighty in this kind of a turn-out."

Indeed, as they passed down the street, all the people cheered them lustily, and the Shaggy Man and the Wizard and the Captain General all took off their hats and bowed politely in acknowledgment.

When they came to the great wall of the Emerald City the gates were opened by the Guardian who always tended them. Over the gateway hung a dull-colored metal magnet shaped like a horse-shoe, placed against a shield of polished gold.

"That," said the Shaggy Man, impressively, "is the wonderful Love Magnet. I brought it to the Emerald City myself, and all who pass beneath this gateway are both loving and beloved."

"It's a fine thing," declared Aunt Em, admiringly. "If we'd had it in Kansas I guess the man who held a mortgage on the farm wouldn't have turned us out."

"Then I'm glad we didn't have it," returned Uncle Henry. "I like Oz better than Kansas, even; an' this little wood Sawhorse beats all the critters I ever saw. He don't have to be curried, or fed, or watered, an' he's strong as an ox. Can he talk, Dorothy?"

"Yes, Uncle," replied the child. "But the Sawhorse never says much. He told me once that he can't talk and think at the same time, so he prefers to think."

"Which is very sensible," declared the Wizard, nodding approvingly. "Which way do we go, Dorothy?"

"Straight ahead into the Quadling Country," she answered. "I've got a letter of interduction to Miss Cuttenclip."

"Oh!" exclaimed the Wizard, much interested. "Are we going there? Then I'm glad I came, for I've always wanted to meet the Cuttenclips."

"Who are they?" inquired Aunt Em.

"Wait till we get there," replied Dorothy, with a laugh; "then you'll see for yourself. I've never seen the Cuttenclips, you know, so I can't 'zactly 'splain 'em to you."

Once free of the Emerald City the Sawhorse dashed away at tremendous speed. Indeed, he

went so fast that Aunt Em had hard work to catch her breath, and Uncle Henry held fast to the seat of the red wagon.

"Gently—gently, my boy!" called the Wizard, and at this the Sawhorse slackened his speed.

"What's wrong?" asked the animal, slightly turning his wooden head to look at the party with one eye, which was a knot of wood.

"Why, we wish to admire the scenery, that's all," answered the Wizard.

"Some of your passengers," added the Shaggy Man, "have never been out of the Emerald City before, and the country is all new to them."

"If you go too fast you'll spoil all the fun," said Dorothy. "There's no hurry."

"Very well; it is all the same to me," observed the Sawhorse; and after that he went at a more moderate pace.

Uncle Henry was astonished.

"How can a wooden thing be so intelligent?" he asked.

"Why, I gave him some sawdust brains the last time I fitted his head with new ears," explained the Wizard. "The sawdust was made from hard knots, and now the Sawhorse is able to think out any knotty problem he meets with."

"I see," said Uncle Henry.

"I don't," remarked Aunt Em; but no one paid any attention to this statement.

Before long they came to a stately building that stood upon a green plain with handsome shade trees grouped here and there.

"What is that?" asked Uncle Henry.

"That," replied the Wizard, "is the Royal Athletic College of Oz, which is directed by Professor H. M. Wogglebug, T. E."

"Let's stop and make a call," suggested Dorothy.

So the Sawhorse drew up in front of the great building and they were met at the door by the learned Wogglebug himself. He seemed fully as tall as the Wizard, and was dressed in a red and white checked vest and a blue swallow-tailed coat, and had yellow knee breeches and purple silk stockings upon his slender legs. A tall hat was jauntily set upon his head and he wore spectacles over his big bright eyes.

"Welcome, Dorothy," said the Wogglebug; "and welcome to all your friends. We are indeed pleased to receive you at this great Temple of Learning."

"I thought it was an Athletic College," said the Shaggy Man.

"It is, my dear sir," answered the Wogglebug, proudly. "Here it is that we teach the youth of our great land scientific College Athletics—in all their purity."

"Don't you teach them anything else?" asked

Dorothy. "Don't they get any reading, writing and 'rithmetic?"

"Oh, yes; of course. They get all those, and more," returned the Professor. "But such things occupy little of their time. Please follow me and I will show you how my scholars are usually occupied. This is a class hour and they are all busy."

They followed him to a big field back of the college building, where several hundred young Ozites were at their classes. In one place they played football, in another baseball. Some played tennis, some golf; some were swimming in a big pool. Upon a river which wound through the grounds several crews in racing boats were rowing with great enthusiasm. Other groups of students played basketball and cricket, while in one place a ring was roped in to permit boxing and wrestling by the energetic youths. All the collegians seemed busy and there was much laughter and shouting.

"This college," said Professor Wogglebug, complacently, "is a great success. Its educational value is undisputed, and we are turning out many great and valuable citizens every year."

"But when do they study?" asked Dorothy.

"Study?" said the Wogglebug, looking perplexed at the question.

"Yes; when do they get their 'rithmetic, and

jogerfy, and such things?"

"Oh, they take doses of those every night and morning," was the reply.

"What do you mean by doses?" Dorothy inquired, wonderingly.

"Why, we use the newly invented School Pills, made by your friend the Wizard. These pills we have found to be very effective, and they save a lot of time. Please step this way and I will show you our Laboratory of Learning."

He led them to a room in the building where many large bottles were standing in rows upon shelves.

"These are the Algebra Pills," said the Professor, taking down one of the bottles. "One at night, on retiring, is equal to four hours of study. Here are the Geography Pills—one at

night and one in the morning. In this next
bottle are the Latin Pills—one three times a day.
Then we have the Grammar Pills—one before
each meal—and the Spelling Pills, which are
taken whenever needed."

"Your scholars must have to take a lot of
pills," remarked Dorothy, thoughtfully. "How
do they take 'em, in applesauce?"

"No, my dear. They are sugar-coated and
are quickly and easily swallowed. I believe the
students would rather take the pills than study,
and certainly the pills are a more effective
method. You see, until these School Pills were
invented we wasted a lot of time in study that
may now be better employed in practising athletics."

"Seems to me the pills are a good thing," said
Omby Amby, who remembered how it used to
make his head ache as a boy to study arithmetic.

"They are, sir," declared the Wogglebug,
earnestly. "They give us an advantage over all
other colleges, because at no loss of time our
boys become thoroughly conversant with Greek
and Latin, Mathematics and Geography, Grammar and Literature. You see they are never
obliged to interrupt their games to acquire the
lesser branches of learning."

"It's a great invention, I'm sure," said Dorothy, looking admiringly at the Wizard, who

blushed modestly at this praise.

"We live in an age of progress," announced Professor Wogglebug, pompously. "It is easier to swallow knowledge than to acquire it laboriously from books. Is it not so, my friends?"

"Some folks can swallow anything," said Aunt Em, "but to me this seems too much like taking medicine."

"Young men in college always have to take their medicine, one way or another," observed the Wizard, with a smile; "and, as our Professor says, these School Pills have proved to be a great success. One day while I was making them I happened to drop one of them, and one of Billina's chickens gobbled it up. A few minutes afterward this chick got upon a roost and recited 'The Boy Stood on the Burning Deck' without making a single mistake. Then it recited 'The Charge of the Light Brigade' and afterwards 'Excelsior.' You see, the chicken had eaten an Elocution Pill."

They now bade good bye to the Professor, and thanking him for his kind reception mounted again into the red wagon and continued their journey.

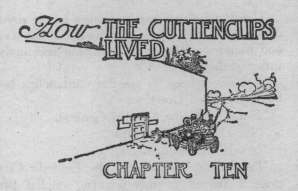

How THE CUTTENCLIPS LIVED

CHAPTER TEN

THE travelers had taken no provisions with them because they knew that they would be welcomed wherever they might go in the Land of Oz, and that the people would feed and lodge them with genuine hospitality. So about noon they stopped at a farmhouse and were given a delicious luncheon of bread and milk, fruits and wheat cakes with maple syrup. After resting a while and strolling through the orchards with their host—a round, jolly farmer—they got into the wagon and again started the Sawhorse along the pretty, winding road.

There were sign-posts at all the corners, and finally they came to one which read:

☛ TAKE THIS ROAD TO THE CUT-
   TENCLIPS

There was also a hand pointing in the right direction, so they turned the Sawhorse that way and found it a very good road, but seemingly little traveled.

"I've never been to see the Cuttenclips before," remarked Dorothy.

"Nor I," said the Captain General.

"Nor I," said the Wizard.

"Nor I," said Billina.

"I've hardly been out of the Emerald City since I arrived in this country," added the Shaggy Man.

"Why, none of us has been there, then," exclaimed the little girl. "I wonder what the Cuttenclips are like."

"We shall soon find out," said the Wizard, with a sly laugh. "I've heard they are rather flimsy things."

The farmhouses became fewer as they proceeded, and the path was at times so faint that the Sawhorse had hard work to keep in the road. The wagon began to jounce, too; so they were obliged to go slowly.

After a somewhat wearisome journey they came in sight of a high wall, painted blue with pink ornaments. This wall was circular, and seemed to enclose a large space. It was so high that only the tops of the trees could be seen above it.

The path led up to a small door in the wall, which was closed and latched. Upon the door was a sign in gold letters reading as follows:

VISITORS are requested to MOVE SLOWLY and CAREFULLY, and to avoid COUGHING or making any BREEZE or DRAUGHT

"That's strange," said the Shaggy Man, reading the sign aloud. "Who *are* the Cuttenclips, anyhow?"

"Why, they're paper dolls," answered Dorothy. "Didn't you know that?"

"Paper dolls! Then let's go somewhere else," said Uncle Henry. "We're all too old to play with dolls, Dorothy."

"But these are different," declared the girl. "They're alive."

"Alive!" gasped Aunt Em, in amazement.

"Yes. Let's go in," said Dorothy.

So they all got out of the wagon, since the door in the wall was not big enough for them to drive the Sawhorse and wagon through it.

"You stay here, Toto!" commanded Dorothy, shaking her finger at the little dog. "You're so careless that you might make a breeze if I let you inside."

Toto wagged his tail as if disappointed at being left behind; but he made no effort to follow them. The Wizard unlatched the door, which opened outward, and they all looked eagerly inside.

Just before the entrance was drawn up a line of tiny soldiers, with uniforms brightly painted and paper guns upon their shoulders. They were exactly alike, from one end of the line to the other, and all were cut out of paper and joined together in the centers of their bodies.

As the visitors entered the enclosure the Wizard let the door swing back into place, and at once the line of soldiers tumbled over, fell flat upon their backs, and lay fluttering upon the ground.

"Hi, there!" called one of them; "what do you mean by slamming the door and blowing us over?"

"I beg your pardon, I'm sure," said the Wizard, regretfully. "I didn't know you were so delicate."

"We're not delicate!" retorted another soldier, raising his head from the ground. "We are strong and healthy; but we can't stand draughts."

"May I help you up?" asked Dorothy.

"If you please," replied the end soldier. "But do it gently, little girl."

Dorothy carefully stood up the line of soldiers, who first dusted their painted clothes and then saluted the visitors with their paper muskets. From the end it was easy to see that the entire line had been cut out of paper, although from the front the soldiers looked rather solid and imposing.

"I've a letter of introduction from Princess Ozma to Miss Cuttenclip," announced Dorothy.

"Very well," said the end soldier, and blew upon a paper whistle that hung around his neck. At once a paper soldier in a Captain's uniform came out of a paper house nearby and approached the group at the entrance. He was not very big, and he walked rather stiffly and uncertainly on his paper legs; but he had a pleasant face, with very red cheeks and very blue eyes, and he bowed so low to the strangers that Dorothy laughed, and the breeze from her mouth nearly blew the Captain over. He wavered and struggled and finally managed to remain upon his feet.

"Take care, Miss!" he said, warningly. "You're breaking the rules, you know, by laughing."

"Oh, I didn't know that," she replied.

"To laugh in this place is nearly as dangerous

as to cough," said the Captain. "You'll have to breathe very quietly, I assure you."

"We'll try to," promised the girl. "May we see Miss Cuttenclip, please?"

"You may," promptly returned the Captain. "This is one of her reception days. Be good enough to follow me."

He turned and led the way up a path, and as they followed slowly, because the paper Captain did not move very swiftly, they took the opportunity to gaze around them at this strange paper country.

Beside the path were paper trees, all cut out very neatly and painted a brilliant green color. And back of the trees were rows of cardboard houses, painted in various colors but most of them having green blinds. Some were large and some small, and in the front yards were beds of paper flowers quite natural in appearance. Over some of the porches paper vines were twined, giving them a cosy and shady look.

As the visitors passed along the street a good many paper dolls came to the doors and windows of their houses to look at them curiously. These dolls were nearly all the same height, but were cut into various shapes, some being fat and some lean. The girl dolls wore many beautiful costumes of tissue paper, making them quite fluffy;

but their heads and hands were no thicker than the paper of which they were made.

Some of the paper people were on the street, walking along or congregated in groups and talking together; but as soon as they saw the strangers they all fluttered into the houses as fast as they could go, so as to be out of danger.

"Excuse me if I go edgewise," remarked the Captain, as they came to a slight hill. "I can get along faster that way and not flutter so much."

"That's all right," said Dorothy. "We don't mind how you go, I'm sure."

At one side of the street was a paper pump, and a paper boy was pumping paper water into a paper pail. The Yellow Hen happened to brush against this boy with her wing, and he flew into the air and fell into a paper tree, where he stuck until the Wizard gently pulled him out. At the same time the pail went soaring into the air, spilling the paper water, while the paper pump bent nearly double.

"Goodness me!" said the Hen. "If I should flop my wings I believe I'd knock over the whole village!"

"Then, don't flop them—please don't!" entreated the Captain. "Miss Cuttenclip would be very much distressed if her village was spoiled."

"Oh, I'll be careful," promised Billina.

"Are not all these paper girls and women named Miss Cuttenclips?" inquired Omby Amby.

"No, indeed," answered the Captain, who was walking better since he began to move edgewise. "There is but one Miss Cuttenclip, who is our Queen, because she made us all. These girls are Cuttenclips, to be sure, but their names are Emily and Polly and Sue and Betty and such things. Only the Queen is called Miss Cuttenclip."

"I must say that this place beats anything I ever heard of," observed Aunt Em. "I used to play with paper dolls myself, an' cut 'em out; but I never thought I'd ever see such things alive."

"I don't see as it's any more curious than hearing hens talk," returned Uncle Henry.

"You're likely to see many queer things in the Land of Oz, sir," said the Wizard. "But a fairy country is extremely interesting when you get used to being surprised."

"Here we are!" called the Captain, stopping before a cottage.

This house was made of wood, and was remarkably pretty in design. In the Emerald City it would have been considered a tiny dwelling, indeed; but in the midst of this paper village it seemed immense. Real flowers were in the garden and real trees grew beside it. Upon the front door was a sign reading:

MISS CUTTENCLIP.

Just as they reached the porch the front door opened and a little girl stood before them. She appeared to be about the same age as Dorothy, and smiling upon her visitors she said, sweetly:

"You are welcome."

All the party seemed relieved to find that here was a real girl, of flesh and blood. She was very dainty and pretty as she stood there welcoming them. Her hair was a golden blonde and her eyes turquoise blue. She had rosy cheeks and lovely white teeth. Over her simple white lawn dress she wore an apron with pink and white checks, and in one hand she held a pair of scissors.

"May we see Miss Cuttenclip, please?" asked Dorothy.

"I am Miss Cuttenclip," was the reply. "Won't you come in?"

She held the door open while they all entered a pretty sitting-room that was littered with all sorts of paper—some stiff, some thin, and some tissue. The sheets and scraps were of all colors.

Upon a table were paints and brushes, while several pair of scissors, of different sizes, were lying about.

"Sit down, please," said Miss Cuttenclip, clearing the paper scraps off some of the chairs. "It is so long since I have had any visitors that I am not properly prepared to receive them. But I'm sure you will pardon my untidy room, for this is my workshop."

"Do you make all the paper dolls?" inquired Dorothy.

"Yes; I cut them out with my scissors, and paint the faces and some of the costumes. It is very pleasant work, and I am happy making my paper village grow."

"But how do the paper dolls happen to be alive?" asked Aunt Em.

"The first dolls I made were not alive," said Miss Cuttenclip. "I used to live near the castle of a great Sorceress named Glinda the Good, and she saw my dolls and said they were very pretty. I told her I thought I would like them better if they were alive, and the next day the Sorceress brought me a lot of magic paper. 'This is live paper,' she said, 'and all the dolls you cut out of it will be alive, and able to think and to talk. When you have used it all up, come to me and I will give you more.'

"Of course I was delighted with this present,"

continued Miss Cuttenclip, "and at once set to work and made several paper dolls, which, as soon as they were cut out, began to walk around and talk to me. But they were so thin that I found that any breeze would blow them over and scatter them dreadfully; so Glinda found this lonely place for me, where few people ever come. She built the wall to keep any wind from blowing away my people, and told me I could build a paper village here and be its Queen. That is why I came here and settled down to work and started the village you now see. It was many years ago that I built the first houses, and I've kept pretty busy and made my village grow finely; and I need not tell you that I am very happy in my work."

"Many years ago!" exclaimed Aunt Em. "Why, how old are you, child?"

"I never keep track of the years," said Miss Cuttenclip, laughing. "You see, I don't grow up at all, but stay just the same as I was when first I came here. Perhaps I'm older even than you are, madam; but I couldn't say for sure."

They looked at the lovely little girl wonderingly, and the Wizard asked:

"What happens to your paper village when it rains?"

"It does not rain here," replied Miss Cuttenclip. "Glinda keeps all the rain storms away; so

I never worry about my dolls getting wet. But now, if you will come with me, it will give me pleasure to show you over my paper kingdom. Of course you must go slowly and carefully, and avoid making any breeze."

They left the cottage and followed their guide through the various streets of the village. It was indeed an amazing place, when one considered that it was all made with scissors, and the visitors were not only greatly interested but full of admiration for the skill of little Miss Cuttenclip.

In one place a large group of especially nice paper dolls assembled to greet their Queen, whom it was easy to see they loved dearly. These dolls marched and danced before the visitors, and then they all waved their paper handkerchiefs and sang in a sweet chorus a song called "The Flag of Our Native Land."

At the conclusion of the song they ran up a handsome paper flag on a tall flagpole, and all of the people of the village gathered around to cheer as loudly as they could—although, of course, their voices were not especially strong.

Miss Cuttenclip was about to make her subjects a speech in reply to this patriotic song, when the Shaggy Man happened to sneeze.

He was a very loud and powerful sneezer at any time, and he had tried so hard to hold in this sneeze that when it suddenly exploded the result was terrible.

The paper dolls were mowed down by dozens, and flew and fluttered in wild confusion in every direction, tumbling this way and that and getting more or less wrinkled and bent.

A wail of terror and grief came from the scattered throng, and Miss Cuttenclip exclaimed:

"Dear me! dear me!" and hurried at once to the rescue of her overturned people.

"Oh, Shaggy Man! How could you?" asked Dorothy, reproachfully.

"I couldn't help it—really I couldn't," protested the Shaggy Man, looking quite ashamed. "And I had no idea it took so little to upset these paper dolls."

"So little!" said Dorothy. "Why, it was 'most as bad as a Kansas cyclone." And then she helped Miss Cuttenclip rescue the paper folk and stand them on their feet again. Two of the cardboard houses had also tumbled over, and the little Queen said she would have to repair them and paste them together before they could be lived in again.

And now, fearing they might do more damage to the flimsy paper people, they decided to go away. But first they thanked Miss Cuttenclip very warmly for her courtesy and kindness to them.

"Any friend of Princess Ozma is always welcome here—unless he sneezes," said the Queen, with a rather severe look at the Shaggy Man, who hung his head. "I like to have visitors admire my wonderful village, and I hope you will call again."

Miss Cuttenclip herself led them to the door in the wall, and as they passed along the street the paper dolls peeped at them half fearfully from the doors and windows. Perhaps they will never forget the Shaggy Man's awful sneeze, and I am sure they were all glad to see the meat people go away.

How THE GENERAL MET THE FIRST AND FOREMOST

CHAPTER ELEVEN

ON leaving the Growleywogs General Guph had to recross the Ripple Lands, and he did not find it a pleasant thing to do. Perhaps having his whiskers pulled out one by one and being used as a pin-cushion for the innocent amusement of a good natured jailor had not improved the quality of Guph's temper, for the old Nome raved and raged at the recollection of the wrongs he had suffered, and vowed to take vengeance upon the Growleywogs after he had used them for his purposes and Oz had been conquered. He went on in this furious way until he was half across the Ripple Land. Then he became seasick, and the rest of the way this naughty Nome was almost as miserable as he deserved to be.

But when he reached the plains again and the ground was firm under his feet he began to feel better, and instead of going back home he turned directly west. A squirrel, perched in a tree, saw him take this road and called to him warningly: "Look out!" But he paid no attention. An eagle paused in its flight through the air to look at him wonderingly and say: "Look out!" But on he went.

No one can say that Guph was not brave, for he had determined to visit those dangerous creatures the Phanfasms, who resided upon the very top of the dread Mountain of Phantastico. The Phanfasms were Erbs, and so dreaded by mortals and immortals alike that no one had been near their mountain home for several thousand years. Yet General Guph hoped to induce them to join in his proposed warfare against the good and happy Oz people.

Guph knew very well that the Phanfasms would be almost as dangerous to the Nomes as they would to the Ozites, but he thought himself so clever that he believed that he could manage these strange creatures and make them obey him. And there was no doubt at all that if he could enlist the services of the Phanfasms their tremendous power, united to the strength of the Growleywogs and the cunning of the Whimsies would doom the Land of Oz to absolute destruction.

So the old Nome climbed the foothills and

trudged along the wild mountain paths until he came to a big gully that encircled the Mountain of Phantastico and marked the boundary line of the dominion of the Phanfasms. This gully was about a third of the way up the mountain, and it was filled to the brim with red-hot molten lava, in which swam fire-serpents and poisonous salamanders. The heat from this mass and its poisonous smell were both so unbearable that even birds hesitated to fly over the gully, but circled around it. All living things kept away from the mountain.

Now Guph had heard, during his long life-time, many tales of these dreaded Phanfasms; so he had heard of this barrier of melted lava, and also he had been told that there was a narrow bridge that spanned it in one place. So he walked along the edge until he found the bridge. It was a single arch of gray stone, and lying flat upon this bridge was a scarlet alligator, seemingly fast asleep.

When Guph stumbled over the rocks in approaching the bridge the creature opened its eyes, from which tiny flames shot in all directions, and after looking at the intruder very wickedly the scarlet alligator closed its eyelids again and lay still.

Guph saw there was no room for him to pass

the alligator on the narrow bridge, so he called out to it:

"Good morning, friend. I don't wish to hurry you, but please tell me if you are coming down, or going up?"

"Neither," snapped the alligator, clicking its cruel jaws together.

The General hesitated.

"Are you likely to stay there long?" he asked.

"A few hundred years or so," said the alligator.

Guph softly rubbed the end of his nose and tried to think what to do.

"Do you know whether the First and Foremost Phanfasm of Phantastico is at home or not?" he presently inquired.

"I expect he is, seeing he is always at home," replied the alligator.

"Ah; who is that coming down the mountain?" asked the Nome, gazing upward.

The alligator turned to look over its shoulder, and at once Guph ran to the bridge and leaped over the sentinel's back before it could turn back again. The scarlet monster made a snap at the Nome's left foot, but missed it by fully an inch.

"Ah ha!" laughed the General, who was now on the mountain path. "I fooled you that time."

"So you did; and perhaps you fooled yourself," retorted the alligator. "Go up the mountain, if you dare, and find out what the First and Foremost will do to you!"

"I will," declared Guph, boldly; and on he went up the path.

At first the scene was wild enough, but gradually it grew more and more awful in appearance. All the rocks had the shapes of frightful beings and even the tree trunks were gnarled and twisted like serpents.

Suddenly there appeared before the Nome a man with the head of an owl. His body was hairy, like that of an ape, and his only clothing was a scarlet scarf twisted around his waist. He bore a huge club in his hand and his round owl eyes blinked fiercely upon the intruder.

"What are you doing here?" he demanded, threatening Guph with his club.

"I've come to see the First and Foremost Phanfasm of Phantastico," replied the General, who did not like the way this creature looked at him, but still was not afraid.

"Ah; you shall see him!" the man said, with a sneering laugh. "The First and Foremost shall decide upon the best way to punish you."

"He will not punish me," returned Guph, calmly, "for I have come here to do him and his people a rare favor. Lead on, fellow, and take me directly to your master."

The owl-man raised his club with a threatening gesture.

"If you try to escape," he said, "beware—"

But here the General interrupted him.

"Spare your threats," said he, "and do not be impertinent, or I will have you severely punished. Lead on, and keep silent!"

This Guph was really a clever rascal, and it seems a pity he was so bad, for in a good cause he might have accomplished much. He realized that he had put himself into a dangerous position by coming to this dreadful mountain, but he also knew that if he showed fear he was lost. So he adopted a bold manner as his best defense. The wisdom of this plan was soon evident, for the Phanfasm with the owl's head turned and led the way up the mountain.

At the very top was a level plain, upon which were heaps of rock that at first glance seemed solid. But on looking closer Guph discovered that these rock heaps were dwellings, for each had an opening.

Not a person was to be seen outside the rock huts. All was silent.

The owl-man led the way among the groups of dwellings to one standing in the center. It seemed no better and no worse than any of the others. Outside the entrance to this rock heap the guide gave a low wail that sounded like "Lee-ow-ah!"

Suddenly there bounded from the opening another hairy man. This one wore the head of a bear. In his hand he bore a brass hoop. He glared at the stranger in evident surprise.

"Why have you captured this foolish wanderer and brought him here?" he demanded, addressing the owl-man.

"I did not capture him," was the answer. "He passed the scarlet alligator and came here of his own free will and accord."

The First and Foremost looked at the General.

"Have you tired of life, then?" he asked.

"No, indeed," answered Guph. "I am a Nome, and the Chief General of King Roquat the Red's great army of Nomes. I come of a long-lived race, and I may say that I expect to live a long time yet. Sit down, you Phanfasms—if you can find a seat in this wild haunt—and listen to what I have to say."

With all his knowledge and bravery General Guph did not know that the steady glare from the bear eyes was reading his inmost thoughts as surely as if they had been put into words. He did not know that these despised rock heaps of the Phanfasms were merely deceptions to his own eyes, nor could he guess that he was standing in the midst of one of the most splendid

and luxurious cities ever built by magic power. All that he saw was a barren waste of rock heaps, a hairy man with an owl's head and another with a bear's head. The sorcery of the Phanfasms permitted him to see no more.

Suddenly the First and Foremost swung his brass hoop and caught Guph around the neck with it. The next instant, before the General could think what had happened to him, he was dragged inside the rock hut. Here, his eyes still blinded to realities, he perceived only a dim light, by which the hut seemed as rough and rude inside as it was outside. Yet he had a strange feeling that many bright eyes were fastened upon him and that he stood in a vast and extensive hall.

The First and Foremost now laughed grimly and released his prisoner.

"If you have anything to say that is interesting," he remarked, "speak out, before I strangle you."

So Guph spoke out. He tried not to pay any attention to a strange rustling sound that he heard, as of an unseen multitude drawing near to listen to his words. His eyes could see only the fierce bear-man, and to him he addressed his speech. First he told of his plan to conquer the Land of Oz and plunder the country of its riches and enslave its people, who, being fairies, could not be killed. After relating all this, and telling of the tunnel the Nome King was building, he said he had come to ask the First and Foremost to join the Nomes, with his band of terrible warriors, and help them to defeat the Oz people.

The General spoke very earnestly and impressively, but when he had finished the bear-man began to laugh as if much amused, and his laughter seemed to be echoed by a chorus of merriment from an unseen multitude. Then, for the first time, Guph began to feel a trifle worried.

"Who else has promised to help you?" finally asked the First and Foremost.

"The Whimsies," replied the General.

Again the bear-headed Phanfasm laughed.

"Any others?" he inquired.

"Only the Growleywogs," said Guph.

This answer set the First and Foremost laughing anew.

"What share of the spoils am I to have?" was the next question.

"Anything you like, except King Roquat's Magic Belt," replied Guph.

At this the Phanfasm set up a roar of laughter, which had its echo in the unseen chorus, and the bear-man seemed so amused that he actually rolled upon the ground and shouted with merriment.

"Oh, these blind and foolish Nomes!" he said. "How big they seem to themselves and how small they really are!"

Suddenly he arose and seized Guph's neck with one hairy paw, dragging him out of the hut into the open.

Here he gave a curious wailing cry, and, as if in answer, from all the rocky huts on the mountain-top came flocking a horde of Phanfasms, all with hairy bodies, but wearing heads of various animals, birds and reptiles. All were ferocious and repulsive-looking to the deceived eyes of the Nome, and Guph could not repress a shudder of disgust as he looked upon them.

The First and Foremost slowly raised his arms, and in a twinkling his hairy skin fell from him and he appeared before the astonished Nome as a beautiful woman, clothed in a flowing gown of pink gauze. In her dark hair flowers were entwined, and her face was noble and calm.

At the same instant the entire band of Phanfasms was transformed into a pack of howling wolves, running here and there as they snarled and showed their ugly yellow fangs.

The woman now raised her arms, even as the man-bear had done, and in a twinkling the wolves became crawling lizards, while she herself changed into a huge butterfly.

Guph had only time to cry out in fear and take a step backward to avoid the lizards when another transformation occurred, and all returned instantly to the forms they had originally worn.

Then the First and Foremost, who had resumed his hairy body and bear head, turned to the Nome and asked:

"Do you still demand our assistance?"

"More than ever," answered the General, firmly.

"Then tell me: what can you offer the Phanfasms that they have not already?" inquired the First and Foremost.

Guph hesitated. He really did not know what to say. The Nome King's vaunted Magic Belt seemed a poor thing compared to the astonishing magical powers of these people. Gold, jewels and slaves they might secure in any quantity without especial effort. He felt that he was dealing with powers greatly beyond him. There was but one argument that might influence the Phanfasms, who were creatures of evil.

"Permit me to call your attention to the exquisite joy of making the happy unhappy," said he at last. "Consider the pleasure of destroying innocent and harmless people."

"Ah! you have answered me," cried the First and Foremost. "For that reason alone we will aid you. Go home, and tell your bandy-legged king that as soon as his tunnel is finished the Phanfasms will be with him and lead his legions to the conquest of Oz. The deadly desert alone has kept us from destroying Oz long ago, and your underground tunnel is a clever thought. Go home, and prepare for our coming!"

Guph was very glad to be permitted to go with this promise. The owl-man led him back down the mountain path and ordered the scarlet alligator to crawl away and allow the Nome to cross the bridge in safety.

After the visitor had gone a brilliant and gorgeous city appeared upon the mountain top, clearly visible to the eyes of the gaily dressed multitude of Phanfasms that lived there. And the First and Foremost, beautifully arrayed, addressed the others in these words:

"It is time we went into the world and brought sorrow and dismay to its people. Too long have we remained by ourselves upon this mountain top, for while we are thus secluded many nations have grown happy and prosperous, and the chief joy of the race of Phanfasms is to destroy happiness. So I think it is lucky that this messenger from the Nomes arrived among us just now, to remind us that the opportunity has come for us to make trouble. We will use King Roquat's tunnel to conquer the Land of Oz. Then we will destroy the Whimsies, the Growleywogs and the Nomes, and afterward go out to ravage and annoy and grieve the whole world."

The multitude of evil Phanfasms eagerly applauded this plan, which they fully approved.

I am told that the Erbs are the most powerful and merciless of all the evil spirits, and the Phanfasms of Phantastico belong to the race of Erbs.

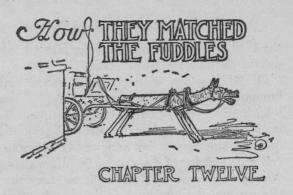

How THEY MATCHED THE FUDDLES

CHAPTER TWELVE

DOROTHY and her fellow travelers rode away from the Cuttenclip village and followed the indistinct path as far as the sign-post. Here they took the main road again and proceeded pleasantly through the pretty farming country. When evening came they stopped at a dwelling and were joyfully welcomed and given plenty to eat and good beds for the night.

Early next morning, however, they were up and eager to start, and after a good breakfast they bade their host good-bye and climbed into the red wagon, to which the Sawhorse had been hitched all night. Being made of wood, this horse never got tired nor cared to lie down. Dorothy was not quite sure whether he ever slept or not, but it was certain that he never did when anybody was around.

The weather is always beautiful in Oz, and

this morning the air was cool and refreshing and the sunshine brilliant and delightful.

In about an hour they came to a place where another road branched off. There was a sign-post here which read:

☛ THIS WAY TO FUDDLECUMJIG

"Oh, here is where we turn," said Dorothy, observing the sign.

"What! Are we going to Fuddlecumjig?" asked the Captain General.

"Yes; Ozma thought we would enjoy the Fuddles. They are said to be very interesting," she replied.

"No one would suspect it from their name," said Aunt Em. "Who are they, anyhow? More paper things?"

"I think not," answered Dorothy, laughing; "but I can't say 'zactly, Aunt Em, what they are. We'll find out when we get there."

"Perhaps the Wizard knows," suggested Uncle Henry.

"No; I've never been there before," said the Wizard. "But I've often heard of Fuddlecumjig and the Fuddles, who are said to be the most peculiar people in all the Land of Oz."

"In what way?" asked the Shaggy Man.

"I don't know, I'm sure," said the Wizard.

Just then, as they rode along the pretty green lane toward Fuddlecumjig, they espied a kangaroo sitting by the roadside. The poor animal had its face covered with both its front paws and was crying so bitterly that the tears coursed down its cheeks in two tiny streams and trickled across the road, where they formed a pool in a small hollow.

The Sawhorse stopped short at this pitiful sight, and Dorothy cried out, with ready sympathy:

"What's the matter, Kangaroo?"

"Boo-hoo! Boo-hoo!" wailed the kangaroo; "I've lost my mi—mi—mi—Oh, boo-hoo! Boo-hoo!"—

"Poor thing," said the Wizard, "she's lost her mister. It's probably her husband, and he's dead."

"No, no, no!" sobbed the kangaroo. "It—it isn't that. I've lost my mi—mi— Oh, boo, boo-hoo!"

"I know," said the Shaggy Man; "she's lost her mirror."

"No; it's my mi—mi—mi—Boo-hoo! My mi— Oh, Boo-hoo!" and the kangaroo cried harder than ever.

"It must be her mince-pie," suggested Aunt Em.

"Or her milk-toast," proposed Uncle Henry.

"I've lost my mi—mi—mittens!" said the kangaroo, getting it out at last.

"Oh!" cried the Yellow Hen, with a cackle of relief. "Why didn't you say so before?"

"Boo-hoo! I—I—couldn't," answered the kangaroo.

"But, see here," said Dorothy, "you don't need mittens in this warm weather."

"Yes, indeed I do," replied the animal, stopping her sobs and removing her paws from her face to look at the little girl reproachfully. "My hands will get all sunburned and tanned without my mittens, and I've worn them so long that I'll probably catch cold without them."

"Nonsense!" said Dorothy. "I never heard before of any kangaroo wearing mittens."

"Didn't you?" asked the animal, as if surprised.

"Never!" repeated the girl. "And you'll probably make yourself sick if you don't stop crying. Where do you live?"

"About two miles beyond Fuddlecumjig," was the answer. "Grandmother Gnit made me the mittens, and she's one of the Fuddles."

"Well, you'd better go home now, and perhaps the old lady will make you another pair," suggested Dorothy. "We're on our way to Fuddlecumjig, and you may hop along beside us."

So they rode on, and the kangaroo hopped beside the red wagon and seemed quickly to have forgotten her loss. By and by the Wizard said to the animal:

"Are the Fuddles nice people?"

"Oh, very nice," answered the kangaroo; "that is, when they're properly put together. But they get dreadfully scattered and mixed up, at times, and then you can't do anything with them."

"What do you mean by their getting scattered?" inquired Dorothy.

"Why, they're made in a good many small pieces," explained the kangaroo; "and whenever any stranger comes near them they have a habit of falling apart and scattering themselves around. That's when they get so dreadfully mixed, and it's a hard puzzle to put them together again."

"Who usually puts them together?" asked Omby Amby.

"Any one who is able to match the pieces. I sometimes put Grandmother Gnit together myself, because I know her so well I can tell every piece that belongs to her. Then, when she's all matched, she knits for me, and that's how she made my mittens. But it took a good many days hard knitting, and I had to put Grandmother together a good many times, because every time I came near she'd scatter herself."

"I should think she would get used to your coming, and not be afraid," said Dorothy.

"It isn't that," replied the kangaroo. "They're not a bit afraid, when they're put together, and usually they're very jolly and pleasant. It's just a habit they have, to scatter themselves, and if they didn't do it they wouldn't be Fuddles."

The travelers thought upon this quite seriously for a time, while the Sawhorse continued to carry them rapidly forward. Then Aunt Em remarked:

"I don't see much use our visitin' these Fuddles. If we find them scattered, all we can do is to sweep 'em up, and then go about our business."

"Oh, I b'lieve we'd better go on," replied Dorothy. "I'm getting hungry, and we must try to get some luncheon at Fuddlecumjig. Perhaps the food won't be scattered as badly as the people."

"You'll find plenty to eat there," declared the kangaroo, hopping along in big bounds because the Sawhorse was going so fast; "and they have a fine cook, too, if you can manage to put him together. There's the town now—just ahead of us!"

They looked ahead and saw a group of very pretty houses standing in a green field a little apart from the main road.

"Some Munchkins came here a few days ago and matched a lot of people together," said the kangaroo. "I think they are together yet, and if you go softly, without making any noise, perhaps they won't scatter."

"Let's try it," suggested the Wizard.

So they stopped the Sawhorse and got out of the wagon, and, after bidding good bye to the kangaroo, who hopped away home, they entered the field and very cautiously approached the group of houses.

So silently did they move that soon they saw through the windows of the houses, people moving around, while others were passing to and fro in the yards between the buildings. They seemed much like other people, from a distance, and apparently they did not notice the little party so quietly approaching.

They had almost reached the nearest house when Toto saw a large beetle crossing the path and barked loudly at it. Instantly a wild clatter was heard from the houses and yards. Dorothy thought it sounded like a sudden hailstorm, and the visitors, knowing that caution was no longer necessary, hurried forward to see what had happened.

After the clatter an intense stillness reigned in the town. The strangers entered the first house they came to, which was also the largest, and found the floor strewn with pieces of the people who lived there. They looked much like fragments of wood neatly painted, and were of all sorts of curious and fantastic shapes, no two pieces being in any way alike.

They picked up some of these pieces and looked at them carefully. On one which Dorothy held was an eye, which looked at her pleasantly but with an interested expression, as if it wondered what she was going to do with it. Quite near by she discovered and picked up a nose, and by matching the two pieces together found that they were part of a face.

"If I could find the mouth," she said, "this Fuddle might be able to talk, and tell us what to do next."

"Then let us find it," replied the Wizard, and

so all got down on their hands and knees and began examining the scattered pieces.

"I've found it!" cried the Shaggy Man, and ran to Dorothy with a queer-shaped piece that had a mouth on it. But when they tried to fit it to the eye and nose they found the parts wouldn't match together.

"That mouth belongs to some other person," said Dorothy. "You see we need a curve here and a point there, to make it fit the face."

"Well, it must be here some place," declared the Wizard; "so if we search long enough we shall find it."

Dorothy fitted an ear on next, and the ear had a little patch of red hair above it. So while the others were searching for the mouth she hunted for pieces with red hair, and found several of them which, when matched to the other pieces, formed the top of a man's head. She had also found the other eye and the ear by the time Omby Amby in a far corner discovered the mouth. When the face was thus completed all parts joined together with a nicety that was astonishing.

"Why, it's like a picture puzzle!" exclaimed the little girl. "Let's find the rest of him, and get him all together."

"What's the rest of him like?" asked the Wizard. "Here are some pieces of blue legs and green arms, but I don't know whether they are his or not."

"Look for a white shirt and a white apron," said the head which had been put together, speaking in a rather faint voice. "I'm the cook."

"Oh, thank you," said Dorothy. "It's lucky we started you first, for I'm hungry, and you can be cooking something for us to eat while we match the other folks together."

It was not so very difficult, now that they had a hint as to how the man was dressed, to find the other pieces belonging to him, and as all of them now worked on the cook, trying piece after piece to see if it would fit, they finally had the cook set up complete.

When he was finished he made them a low bow and said:

"I will go at once to the kitchen and prepare your dinner. You will find it something of a job to get all the Fuddles together, so I advise you to begin on the Lord High Chigglewitz, whose first name is Larry. He's a bald-headed fat man and is dressed in a blue coat with brass buttons, a pink vest and drab breeches. A piece of his left knee is missing, having been lost years ago when he scattered himself too carelessly. That makes him limp a little, but he gets along very well with half a knee. As he is the chief personage in this town of Fuddlecumjig, he will be able to welcome you and assist you with the others. So it will be best to work on him while I'm getting your dinner."

"We will," said the Wizard; "and thank you very much, cook, for the suggestion."

Aunt Em was the first to discover a piece of the Lord High Chigglewitz.

"It seems to me like a fool business, this matching folks together," she remarked; "but as we haven't anything to do till dinner's ready we may as well get rid of some of this rubbish. Here, Henry, get busy and look for Larry's bald head. I've got his pink vest, all right."

They worked with eager interest, and Billina proved a great help to them. The Yellow Hen had sharp eyes and could put her head close to the various pieces that lay scattered around. She would examine the Lord High Chigglewitz and see which piece of him was next needed, and then hunt around until she found it. So before an hour had passed old Larry was standing complete before them.

"I congratulate you, my friends," he said, speaking in a cheerful voice. "You are certainly the cleverest people who ever visited us. I was never matched together so quickly in my life. I'm considered a great puzzle, usually."

"Well," said Dorothy, "there used to be a picture puzzle craze in Kansas, and so I've had some 'sperience matching puzzles. But the pictures were flat, while you are round, and that makes you harder to figure out."

"Thank you, my dear," replied old Larry, greatly pleased. "I feel highly complimented. Were I not a really good puzzle there would be no object in my scattering myself."

"Why do you do it?" asked Aunt Em, severely. "Why don't you behave yourself, and stay put together?"

The Lord High Chigglewitz seemed annoyed by this speech; but he replied, politely:

"Madam, you have perhaps noticed that every person has some peculiarity. Mine is to scatter myself. What your own peculiarity is I will not venture to say; but I shall never find fault with you, whatever you do."

"Now, you've got your diploma, Em," said Uncle Henry, with a laugh, "and I'm glad of it. This is a queer country, and we may as well take people as we find them."

"If we did, we'd leave these folks scattered," she returned, and this retort made everybody laugh good-naturedly.

Just then Omby Amby found a hand with a knitting needle in it, and they decided to put Grandmother Gnit together. She proved an easier puzzle than old Larry, and when she was completed they found her a pleasant old lady who welcomed them cordially. Dorothy told her how the kangaroo had lost her mittens, and Grandmother Gnit promised to set to work at once and make the poor animal another pair.

Then the cook came to call them to dinner, and they found an inviting meal prepared for them. The Lord High Chigglewitz sat at the head of the table and Grandmother Gnit at the

foot, and the guests had a merry time and thoroughly enjoyed themselves.

After dinner they went out into the yard and matched several other people together, and this work was so interesting that they might have spent the entire day at Fuddlecumjig had not the Wizard suggested that they resume their journey.

"But I don't like to leave all these poor people

scattered," said Dorothy, undecided what to do.

"Oh, don't mind us, my dear," returned old Larry. "Every day or so some of the Gillikins, or Munchkins, or Winkies come here to amuse themselves by matching us together, so there will be no harm in leaving these pieces where they are for a time. But I hope you will visit us again, and if you do you will always be welcome, I assure you."

"Don't you ever match each other?" she inquired.

"Never; for we are no puzzles to ourselves, and so there wouldn't be any fun in it."

They now said goodbye to the queer Fuddles and got into their wagon to continue their journey.

"Those are certainly strange people," remarked Aunt Em, thoughtfully, as they drove away from Fuddlecumjig, "but I really can't see what use they are, at all."

"Why, they amused us all for several hours," replied the Wizard. "That is being of use to us, I'm sure."

"I think they're more fun than playing solitaire or mumbletypeg," declared Uncle Henry, soberly. "For my part, I'm glad we visited the Fuddles."

How THE GENERAL TALKED TO THE KING

CHAPTER THIRTEEN

WHEN General Guph returned to the cavern of the Nome King his Majesty asked:

"Well, what luck? Will the Whimsies join us?"

"They will," answered the General. "They will fight for us with all their strength and cunning."

"Good!" exclaimed the King. "What reward did you promise them?"

"Your Majesty is to use the Magic Belt to give each Whimsie a large, fine head, in place of the small one he is now obliged to wear."

"I agree to that," said the King. "This is good news, Guph, and it makes me feel more certain of the conquest of Oz."

"But I have other news for you," announced the General.

138

"Good or bad?"

"Good, your Majesty."

"Then I will hear it," said the King, with interest.

"The Growleywogs will join us."

"No!" cried the astonished King.

"Yes, indeed," said the General. "I have their promise."

"But what reward do they demand?" inquired the King, suspiciously, for he knew how greedy the Growleywogs were.

"They are to take a few of the Oz people for their slaves," replied Guph. He did not think it necessary to tell Roquat that the Growleywogs demanded twenty thousand slaves. It would be time enough for that when Oz was conquered.

"A very reasonable request, I'm sure," remarked the King. "I must congratulate you, Guph, upon the wonderful success of your journey."

"But that is not all," said the General, proudly.

The King seemed astonished.

"Speak out, sir!" he commanded.

"I have seen the First and Foremost Phanfasm of the Mountain of Phantastico, and he will bring his people to assist us."

"What!" cried the King. "The Phanfasms! You don't mean it, Guph!"

"It is true," declared the General, proudly. The King became thoughtful, and his brows wrinkled.

"I'm afraid, Guph," he said rather anxiously, "that the First and Foremost may prove as dangerous to us as to the Oz people. If he and his terrible band come down from the mountain they may take the notion to conquer the Nomes!"

"Pah! That is a foolish idea," retorted Guph, irritably, but he knew in his heart that the King was right. "The First and Foremost is a particular friend of mine, and will do us no harm. Why, when I was there, he even invited me into his house."

The General neglected to tell the King how he had been jerked into the hut of the First and Foremost by means of the brass hoop. So Roquat the Red looked at his General admiringly and said:

"You are a wonderful Nome, Guph. I'm sorry I did not make you my General before. But what reward did the First and Foremost demand?"

"Nothing at all," answered Guph. "Even the Magic Belt itself could not add to his powers of sorcery. All the Phanfasms wish is to destroy the Oz people, who are good and happy. This pleasure will amply repay them for assisting us."

"When will they come?" asked Roquat, half fearfully.

"When the tunnel is completed," said the General.

"We are nearly half way under the desert now," announced the King; "and that is fast work, because the tunnel has to be drilled through solid rock. But after we have passed the desert it will not take us long to extend the tunnel to the walls of the Emerald City."

"Well, whenever you are ready, we shall be joined by the Whimsies, the Growleywogs and the Phanfasms," said Guph; "so the conquest of Oz is assured without a doubt."

Again the King seemed thoughtful.

"I'm almost sorry we did not undertake the conquest alone," said he. "All of these allies are dangerous people, and they may demand more than you have promised them. It might have been better to have conquered Oz without any outside assistance."

"We could not do it," said the General, positively.

"Why not, Guph?"

"You know very well. You have had one experience with the Oz people, and they defeated you."

"That was because they rolled eggs at us,"

replied the King, with a shudder. "My Nomes cannot stand eggs, any more than I can myself. They are poison to all who live underground."

"That is true enough," agreed Guph.

"But we might have taken the Oz people by surprise, and conquered them before they had a chance to get any eggs. Our former defeat was due to the fact that the girl Dorothy had a Yel-

low Hen with her. I do not know what ever became of that hen, but I believe there are no hens at all in the Land of Oz, and so there could be no eggs there."

"On the contrary," said Guph, "there are now hundreds of chickens in Oz, and they lay heaps of those dangerous eggs. I met a goshawk on my way home, and the bird informed me that he had lately been to Oz to capture and devour some of the young chickens. But they are protected by magic, so the hawk did not get a single one of them."

"That is a very bad report," said the King, nervously. "Very bad, indeed. My Nomes are willing to fight, but they simply can't face hen's eggs—and I don't blame them."

"They won't need to face them," replied Guph. "I'm afraid of eggs myself, and don't propose to take any chances of being poisoned by them. My plan is to send the Whimsies through the tunnel first, and then the Growleywogs and the Phanfasms. By the time we Nomes get there the eggs will all be used up, and we may then pursue and capture the inhabitants at our leisure."

"Perhaps you are right," returned the King, with a dismal sigh. "But I want it distinctly understood that I claim Ozma and Dorothy as my own prisoners. They are rather nice girls, and I do not intend to let any of those dreadful creatures hurt them, or make them their slaves. When I have captured them I will bring them here and transform them into china ornaments to stand on my mantle. They will look very pretty—Dorothy on one end of the mantle and Ozma on the other—and I shall take great care to see they are not broken when the maids dust them."

"Very well, your Majesty. Do what you will with the girls, for all I care. Now that our plans are arranged, and we have the three most powerful bands of evil spirits in the world to assist us, let us make haste to get the tunnel finished as soon as possible."

"It will be ready in three days," promised the King, and hurried away to inspect the work and see that the Nomes kept busy.

CHAPTER FOURTEEN

"WHERE next?" asked the Wizard, when they had left the town of Fuddlecumjig and the Saw-horse had started back along the road.

"Why, Ozma laid out this trip," replied Dorothy, "and she 'vised us to see the Rigmaroles next, and then visit the Tin Woodman."

"That sounds good," said the Wizard. "But what road do we take to get to the Rigmaroles?"

"I don't know, 'zactly," returned the little girl; "but it must be somewhere just southwest from here."

"Then why need we go back to the cross-roads?" asked the Shaggy Man. "We might save a lot of time by branching off here."

"There isn't any path," asserted Uncle Henry.

"Then we'd better go back to the signposts, and make sure of our way," decided Dorothy.

But after they had gone a short distance

145

farther the Sawhorse, who had overheard their conversation, stopped and said:

"Here is a path."

Sure enough, a dim path seemed to branch off from the road they were on, and it led across pretty green meadows and past leafy groves, straight toward the southwest.

"That looks like a good path," said Omby Amby. "Why not try it?"

"All right," answered Dorothy. "I'm anxious to see what the Rigmaroles are like, and this path ought to take us there the quickest way."

No one made any objection to the plan, so the Sawhorse turned into the path, which proved to be nearly as good as the one they had taken to get to the Fuddles.

At first they passed a few retired farmhouses, but soon these scattered dwellings were left behind and only the meadows and the trees were before them. But they rode along in cheerful contentment, and Aunt Em got into an argument with Billina about the proper way to raise chickens.

"I do not care to contradict you," said the Yellow Hen, with dignity, "but I have an idea I know more about chickens than human beings do."

"Pshaw!" replied Aunt Em, "I've raised chickens for nearly forty years, Billina, and I know you've got to starve 'em to make 'em lay lots of eggs, and stuff 'em if you want good broilers."

"Broilers!" exclaimed Billina, in horror. "Broil my chickens!"

"Why, that's what they're for, ain't it?" asked Aunt Em, astonished.

"No, Aunt, not in Oz," said Dorothy. "People do not eat chickens here. You see, Billina was the first hen that was ever seen in this country, and I brought her here myself. Everybody liked her an' respected her, so the Oz people wouldn't any more eat her chickens than they would eat Billina."

"Well, I declare," gasped Aunt Em. "How about the eggs?"

"Oh, if we have more eggs than we want to hatch, we allow people to eat them," said Billina. "Indeed, I am very glad the Oz folks like our eggs, for otherwise they would spoil."

"This certainly is a queer country," sighed Aunt Em.

"Excuse me," called the Sawhorse, "the path has ended and I'd like to know which way to go."

They looked around and, sure enough, there was no path to be seen.

"Well," said Dorothy, "we're going southwest, and it seems just as easy to follow that direction without a path as with one."

"Certainly," answered the Sawhorse. "It is not hard to draw the wagon over the meadow. I only want to know where to go."

"There's a forest over there across the prairie," said the Wizard, "and it lies in the direction we are going. Make straight for the forest, Sawhorse, and you're bound to go right."

So the wooden animal trotted on again and the meadow grass was so soft under the wheels that it made easy riding. But Dorothy was a little uneasy at losing the path, because now there was nothing to guide them.

No houses were to be seen at all, so they could not ask their way of any farmer; and although the Land of Oz was always beautiful, wherever one might go, this part of the country was strange to all the party.

"Perhaps we're lost," suggested Aunt Em, after they had proceeded quite a way in silence.

"Never mind," said the Shaggy Man; "I've been lost many a time—and so has Dorothy—and we've always been found again."

"But we may get hungry," remarked Omby Amby. "That is the worst of getting lost in a place where there are no houses near."

"We had a good dinner at the Fuddle town," said Uncle Henry, "and that will keep us from starving to death for a long time."

"No one ever starved to death in Oz," declared Dorothy, positively; "but people may get pretty hungry sometimes."

The Wizard said nothing, and he did not seem especially anxious. The Sawhorse was trotting along briskly, yet the forest seemed farther away than they had thought when they first saw it. So it was nearly sundown when they finally came to the trees; but now they found themselves in a most beautiful spot, the wide-spreading trees being covered with flowering vines and having soft mosses underneath them.

"This will be a good place to camp," said the Wizard, as the Sawhorse stopped for further instructions.

"Camp!" they all echoed.

"Certainly," asserted the Wizard. "It will be dark before very long and we cannot travel through this forest at night. So let us make a camp here, and have some supper, and sleep until daylight comes again."

They all looked at the little man in astonishment, and Aunt Em said, with a sniff:

"A pretty camp we'll have, I must say! I suppose you intend us to sleep under the wagon."

"And chew grass for our supper," added the Shaggy Man, laughing.

But Dorothy seemed to have no doubts and was quite cheerful.

"It's lucky we have the wonderful Wizard with us," she said; "because he can do 'most anything he wants to."

"Oh, yes; I forgot we had a Wizard," said Uncle Henry, looking at the little man curiously.

"I didn't," chirped Billina, contentedly.

The Wizard smiled and climbed out of the wagon, and all the others followed him.

"In order to camp," said he, "the first thing we need is tents. Will some one please lend me a handkerchief?"

The Shaggy Man offered him one, and Aunt Em another. He took them both and laid them carefully upon the grass near to the edge of the forest. Then he laid his own handkerchief down, too, and standing a little back from them he waved his left hand toward the handkerchiefs and said:

"Tents of canvas, white as snow,
Let me see how fast you grow!"

Then, lo and behold! the handkerchiefs became tiny tents, and as the travelers looked at them the tents grew bigger and bigger until in a few minutes each one was large enough to contain the entire party.

"This," said the Wizard, pointing to the first tent, "is for the accommodation of the ladies.

Dorothy, you and your Aunt may step inside and take off your things."

Every one ran to look inside the tent, and they saw two pretty white beds, all ready for Dorothy and Aunt Em, and a silver roost for Billina. Rugs were spread upon the grassy floor and some camp chairs and a table completed the furniture.

"Well, well, well! This beats anything I ever saw or heard of!" exclaimed Aunt Em, and she glanced at the Wizard almost fearfully, as if he might be dangerous because of his great powers.

"Oh, Mr. Wizard! How did you manage to do it?" asked Dorothy.

"It's a trick Glinda the Sorceress taught me, and it is much better magic than I used to practise in Omaha, or when I first came to Oz," he answered. "When the Good Glinda found I was to live in the Emerald City always, she promised to help me, because she said the Wizard of Oz ought really to be a clever Wizard, and not a humbug. So we have been much together and I am learning so fast that I expect to be able to accomplish some really wonderful things in time."

"You've done it now!" declared Dorothy. "These tents are just wonderful!"

"But come and see the men's tent," said the Wizard. So they went to the second tent, which had shaggy edges because it had been made from the Shaggy Man's handkerchief, and found that completely furnished also. It contained four neat beds for Uncle Henry, Omby Amby, the Shaggy Man and the Wizard. Also there was a soft rug for Toto to lie upon.

"The third tent," explained the Wizard, "is our dining room and kitchen."

They visited that next, and found a table and dishes in the dining tent, with plenty of those things necessary to use in cooking. The Wizard carried out a big kettle and set it swinging on a crossbar before the tent. While he was doing this Omby Amby and the Shaggy Man brought a supply of twigs from the forest and then they built a fire underneath the kettle.

"Now, Dorothy," said the Wizard, smiling, "I expect you to cook our supper."

"But there is nothing in the kettle," she cried.

"Are you sure?" inquired the Wizard.

"I didn't see anything put in, and I'm almost sure it was empty when you brought it out," she replied.

"Nevertheless," said the little man, winking slyly at Uncle Henry, "you will do well to watch our supper, my dear, and see that it doesn't boil over."

Then the men took some pails and went into the forest to search for a spring of water, and while they were gone Aunt Em said to Dorothy:

"I believe the Wizard is fooling us. I saw the kettle myself, and when he hung it over the fire there wasn't a thing in it but air."

"Don't worry," remarked Billina, confidently, as she nestled in the grass before the fire. "You'll find something in the kettle when it's taken off— and it won't be poor, innocent chickens, either."

"Your hen has very bad manners, Dorothy,"

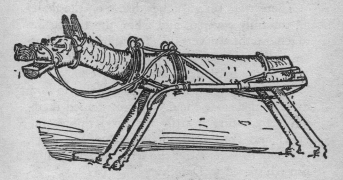

said Aunt Em, looking somewhat disdainfully at Billina. "It seems too bad she ever learned how to talk."

There might have been another unpleasant quarrel between Aunt Em and Billina had not the men returned just then with their pails filled with clear, sparkling water. The Wizard told Dorothy that she was a good cook and he believed their supper was ready.

So Uncle Henry lifted the kettle from the fire and poured its contents into a big platter which the Wizard held for him. The platter was fairly heaped with a fine stew, smoking hot, with many kinds of vegetables and dumplings and a rich, delicious gravy.

The Wizard triumphantly placed the platter upon the table in the dining tent and then they all sat down in camp chairs to the feast.

There were several other dishes on the table, all carefully covered, and when the time came to remove these covers they found bread and butter, cakes, cheese, pickles and fruits—including some of the luscious strawberries of Oz.

No one ventured to ask a question as to how these things came there. They contented themselves by eating heartily the good things provided, and Toto and Billina had their full share, you may be sure. After the meal was over Aunt Em whispered to Dorothy:

"That may have been magic food, my dear, and for that reason perhaps it won't be very nourishing; but I'm willing to say it tasted as good as anything I ever et." Then she added, in a louder tone: "Who's going to do the dishes?"

"No one, madam," answered the Wizard. "The dishes have 'done' themselves."

"La sakes!" ejaculated the good lady, holding up her hands in amazement. For, sure enough, when she looked at the dishes they had a moment before left upon the table, she found them all washed and dried and piled up into neat stacks.

How DOROTHY HAPPENED TO GET LOST

CHAPTER FIFTEEN

IT was a beautiful evening, so they drew their camp chairs in a circle before one of the tents and began to tell stories to amuse themselves and pass away the time before they went to bed.

Pretty soon a zebra was seen coming out of the forest, and he trotted straight up to them and said politely:

"Good evening, people."

The zebra was a sleek little animal and had a slender head, a stubby mane and a paint-brush tail—very like a donkey's. His neatly shaped white body was covered with regular bars of dark brown, and his hoofs were delicate as those of a deer.

"Good evening, friend Zebra," said Omby Amby, in reply to the creature's greeting. "Can we do anything for you?"

"Yes," answered the zebra. "I should like you

to settle a dispute that has long been a bother
to me, as to whether there is more water or land
in the world."

"Who are you disputing with?" asked the
Wizard.

"With a soft-shell crab," said the zebra. "He
lives in a pool where I go to drink every day,
and he is a very impertinent crab, I assure you.
I have told him many times that the land is
much greater in extent than the water, but he
will not be convinced. Even this very evening,
when I told him he was an insignificant creature
who lived in a small pool, he asserted that the
water was greater and more important than the
land. So, seeing your camp, I decided to ask you
to settle the dispute for once and all, that I may
not be further annoyed by this ignorant crab."

When they had listened to this explanation
Dorothy inquired:

"Where is the soft-shell crab?"

"Not far away," replied the zebra. "If you will
agree to judge between us I will run and get
him."

"Run along, then," said the little girl.

So the animal pranced into the forest and
soon came trotting back to them. When he drew
near they found a soft-shell crab clinging fast to
the stiff hair of the zebra's head, where it held
on by one claw.

"Now then, Mr. Crab," said the zebra, "here are the people I told you about; and they know more than you do, who live in a pool, and more than I do, who live in a forest. For they have been travelers all over the world, and know every part of it."

"There's more of the world than Oz," declared the crab, in a stubborn voice.

"That is true," said Dorothy; "but I used to live in Kansas, in the United States, and I've been to California and to Australia—and so has Uncle Henry."

"For my part," added the Shaggy Man, "I've been to Mexico and Boston and many other foreign countries."

"And I," said the Wizard, "have been to Europe and Ireland."

"So you see," continued the zebra, addressing the crab, "here are people of real consequence, who know what they are talking about."

"Then they know there's more water in the world than there is land," asserted the crab, in a shrill, petulant voice.

"They know you are wrong to make such an absurd statement, and they will probably think you are a lobster instead of a crab," retorted the animal.

At this taunt the crab reached out its other claw and seized the zebra's ear, and the creature gave a cry of pain and began prancing up and down, trying to shake off the crab, which clung fast.

"Stop pinching!" cried the zebra. "You promised not to pinch if I would carry you here!"

"And you promised to treat me respectfully," said the crab, letting go the ear.

"Well, haven't I?" demanded the zebra.

"No; you called me a lobster," said the crab.

"Ladies and gentlemen," continued the zebra, "please pardon my poor friend, because he is ignorant and stupid, and does not understand. Also the pinch of his claw is very annoying. So pray tell him that the world contains more land than water, and when he has heard your judgment I will carry him back and dump him into his pool, where I hope he will be more modest in the future."

"But we cannot tell him that," said Dorothy, gravely, "because it would not be true."

"What!" exclaimed the zebra, in astonishment; "do I hear you aright?"

"The soft-shell crab is correct," declared the Wizard. "There is considerably more water than there is land in the world."

"Impossible!" protested the zebra. "Why, I can run for days upon the land, and find but little water."

"Did you ever see an ocean?" asked Dorothy.

"Never," admitted the zebra. "There is no such thing as an ocean in the Land of Oz."

"Well, there are several oceans in the world," said Dorothy, "and people sail in ships upon these oceans for weeks and weeks, and never see a bit of land at all. And the joggerfys will tell you that all the oceans put together are bigger than all the land put together."

At this the crab began laughing in queer chuckles that reminded Dorothy of the way Billina sometimes cackled.

"*Now* will you give up, Mr. Zebra?" it cried, jeeringly; "now will you give up?"

The zebra seemed much humbled.

"Of course I cannot read geographys," he said.

"You could take one of the Wizard's School Pills," suggested Billina, "and that would make you learned and wise without studying."

The crab began laughing again, which so provoked the zebra that he tried to shake the little creature off. This resulted in more ear-pinching, and finally Dorothy told them that if they could not behave they must go back to the forest.

"I'm sorry I asked you to decide this question," said the zebra, crossly. "So long as neither of us could prove we were right we quite enjoyed the dispute; but now I can never drink at that pool again without the soft-shell crab laughing at me. So I must find another drinking place."

"Do! Do, you ignoramus!" shouted the crab, as loudly as his little voice would carry. "Rile some other pool with your clumsy hoofs, and let your betters alone after this!"

Then the zebra trotted back to the forest, bearing the crab with him, and disappeared

amid the gloom of the trees. And as it was now getting dark the travelers said good night to one another and went to bed.

Dorothy awoke just as the light was beginning to get strong next morning, and not caring to sleep any later she quietly got out of bed, dressed herself, and left the tent where Aunt Em was yet peacefully slumbering.

Outside she noticed Billina busily pecking around to secure bugs or other food for breakfast, but none of the men in the other tent seemed awake. So the little girl decided to take a walk in the woods and try to discover some path or road that they might follow when they again started upon their journey.

She had reached the edge of the forest when the Yellow Hen came fluttering along and asked where she was going.

"Just to take a walk, Billina; and maybe I'll find some path," said Dorothy.

"Then I'll go along," decided Billina, and scarcely had she spoken when Toto ran up and joined them.

Toto and the Yellow Hen had become quite friendly by this time, although at first they did not get along well together. Billina had been rather suspicious of dogs, and Toto had had an idea that it was every dog's duty to chase a hen on sight. But Dorothy had talked to them and scolded them for not being agreeable to one another until they grew better acquainted and became friends.

I won't say they loved each other dearly, but at least they had stopped quarreling and now managed to get on together very well.

The day was growing lighter every minute

and driving the black shadows out of the forest;
so Dorothy found it very pleasant walking under
the trees. She went some distance in one direction, but not finding a path, presently turned
in a different direction. There was no path here,
either, although she advanced quite a way into
the forest, winding here and there among the
trees and peering through the bushes in an en-
deavor to find some beaten track.

"I think we'd better go back," suggested the
Yellow Hen, after a time. "The people will all
be up by this time and breakfast will be ready."

"Very well," agreed Dorothy. "Let's see—the
camp must be over this way."

She had probably made a mistake about that,
for after they had gone far enough to have
reached the camp they still found themselves
in the thick of the woods. So the little girl
stopped short and looked around her, and Toto
glanced up into her face with his bright little
eyes and wagged his tail as if he knew something was wrong. He couldn't tell much about
direction himself, because he had spent his time
prowling among the bushes and running here
and there; nor had Billina paid much attention
to where they were going, being interested in
picking bugs from the moss as they passed along.
The Yellow Hen now turned one eye up toward
the little girl and asked:

"Have you forgotten where the camp is, Dorothy?"

"Yes," she admitted; "have you, Billina?"

"I didn't try to remember," returned Billina. "I'd no idea you would get lost, Dorothy."

"It's the thing we don't expect, Billina, that usually happens," observed the girl, thoughtfully. "But it's no use standing here. Let's go in that direction," pointing a finger at random. "It may be we'll get out of the forest over there."

So on they went again, but this way the trees were closer together, and the vines were so tangled that often they tripped Dorothy up.

Suddenly a voice cried sharply:

"Halt!"

At first Dorothy could see nothing, although she looked around very carefully. But Billina exclaimed:

"Well, I declare!"

"What is it?" asked the little girl: for Toto began barking at something, and following his gaze she discovered what it was.

A row of spoons had surrounded the three, and these spoons stood straight up on their handles and carried swords and muskets. Their faces were outlined in the polished bowls and they looked very stern and severe.

Dorothy laughed at the queer things.

"Who are you?" she asked.

"We're the Spoon Brigade," said one.

"In the service of his Majesty King Kleaver," said another.

"And you are our prisoners," said a third.

Dorothy sat down on an old stump and looked at them, her eyes twinkling with amusement.

"What would happen," she inquired, "if I should set my dog on your Brigade?"

"He would die," replied one of the spoons, sharply. "One shot from our deadly muskets would kill him, big as he is."

"Don't risk it, Dorothy," advised the Yellow Hen. "Remember this is a fairy country, yet none of us three happens to be a fairy."

Dorothy grew sober at this.

"P'raps you're right, Billina," she answered. "But how funny it is, to be captured by a lot of spoons!"

"I do not see anything very funny about it," declared a spoon. "We're the regular military brigade of the kingdom."

"What kingdom?" she asked.

"Utensia," said he.

"I never heard of it before," asserted Dorothy. Then she added, thoughtfully, "I don't believe Ozma ever heard of Utensia, either. Tell me, are you not subjects of Ozma of Oz?"

"We never have heard of her," retorted a spoon. "We are subjects of King Kleaver, and obey only his orders, which are to bring all prisoners to him as soon as they are captured. So step lively, my girl, and march with us, or we may be tempted to cut off a few of your toes with our swords."

This threat made Dorothy laugh again. She did not believe she was in any danger; but here was a new and interesting adventure, so she was willing to be taken to Utensia that she might see what King Kleaver's kingdom was like.

CHAPTER SIXTEEN

THERE must have been from six to eight dozen spoons in the Brigade, and they marched away in the shape of a hollow square, with Dorothy, Billina and Toto in the center of the square. Before they had gone very far Toto knocked over one of the spoons by wagging his tail, and then the Captain of the Spoons told the little dog to be more careful, or he would be punished. So Toto was careful, and the Spoon Brigade moved along with astonishing swiftness, while Dorothy really had to walk fast to keep up with it.

By and by they left the woods and entered a big clearing, in which was the Kingdom of Utensia.

Standing all around the clearing were a good many cookstoves, ranges and grills, of all sizes and shapes, and besides these there were several kitchen cabinets and cupboards and a few kitchen tables. These things were crowded with utensils of all sorts: frying pans, sauce pans, kettles, forks, knives, basting and soup spoons, nutmeg graters, sifters, colenders, meat saws, flat irons, rolling pins and many other things of a like nature.

When the Spoon Brigade appeared with the prisoners a wild shout arose and many of the utensils hopped off their stoves or their benches and ran crowding around Dorothy and the hen and the dog.

"Stand back!" cried the Captain, sternly, and he led his captives through the curious throng until they came before a big range that stood in the center of the clearing. Beside this range was a butcher's block upon which lay a great cleaver with a keen edge. It rested upon the flat of its back, its legs were crossed and it was smoking a long pipe.

"Wake up, your Majesty," said the Captain. "Here are prisoners."

Hearing this, King Kleaver sat up and looked at Dorothy sharply.

"Gristle and fat!" he cried. "Where did this girl come from?"

"I found her in the forest and brought her here a prisoner," replied the Captain.

"Why did you do that?" inquired the King, puffing his pipe lazily.

"To create some excitement," the Captain answered. "It is so quiet here that we are all getting rusty for want of amusement. For my part, I prefer to see stirring times."

"Naturally," returned the cleaver, with a nod. "I have always said, Captain, without a bit of irony, that you are a sterling officer and a solid citizen, bowled and polished to a degree. But what do you expect me to do with these prisoners?"

"That is for you to decide," declared the Captain. "You are the King."

"To be sure; to be sure," muttered the cleaver, musingly. "As you say, we have had dull times since the steel and grindstone eloped and left us. Command my Counselors and the Royal Courtiers to attend me, as well as the High Priest and the Judge. We'll then decide what can be done."

The Captain saluted and retired and Dorothy sat down on an overturned kettle and asked:

"Have you anything to eat in your kingdom?"

"Here! Get up! Get off from me!" cried a faint voice, at which his Majesty the cleaver said:

"Excuse me, but you're sitting on my friend the Ten-quart Kettle."

Dorothy at once arose, and the kettle turned

right side up and looked at her reproachfully.

"I'm a friend of the King, so no one dares sit on me," said he.

"I'd prefer a chair, anyway," she replied.

"Sit on that hearth," commanded the King.

So Dorothy sat on the hearth-shelf of the big range, and the subjects of Utensia began to gather around in a large and inquisitive throng. Toto lay at Dorothy's feet and Billina flew upon the range, which had no fire in it, and perched there as comfortably as she could.

When all the Counselors and Courtiers had assembled—and these seemed to include most of the inhabitants of the kingdom—the King rapped on the block for order and said:

"Friends and Fellow Utensils! Our worthy Commander of the Spoon Brigade, Captain Dipp, has captured the three prisoners you see before you and brought them here for—for—I don't know what for. So I ask your advice how to act in this matter, and what fate I should mete out to these captives. Judge Sifter, stand on my right. It is your business to sift this affair to the bottom. High Priest Colender, stand on my left and see that no one testifies falsely in this matter."

As these two officials took their places Dorothy asked:

"Why is the colender the High Priest?"

"He's the holiest thing we have in the king-dom," replied King Kleaver.

"Except me," said a sieve. "I'm the whole thing when it comes to holes."

"What we need," remarked the King, rebuk-ingly, "is a wireless sieve. I must speak to Mar-coni about it. These old fashioned sieves talk too much. Now, it is the duty of the King's Counselors to counsel the King at all times of emergency, so I beg you to speak out and advise me what to do with these prisoners."

"I demand that they be killed several times, until they are dead!" shouted a pepperbox, hop-ping around very excitedly.

"Compose yourself, Mr. Paprica," advised the King. "Your remarks are piquant and highly-seasoned, but you need a scattering of common-sense. It is only necessary to kill a person once to make him dead; but I do not see that it is necessary to kill this little girl at all."

"I don't, either," said Dorothy.

"Pardon me, but you are not expected to ad-vise me in this matter," replied King Kleaver.

"Why not?" asked Dorothy.

"You might be prejudiced in your own favor, and so mislead us," he said. "Now then, good subjects, who speaks next?"

"I'd like to smooth this thing over, in some way," said a flatiron, earnestly. "We are supposed to be useful to mankind, you know."

"But the girl isn't mankind! She's woman-kind!" yelled a corkscrew.

"What do you know about it?" inquired the King.

"I'm a lawyer," said the corkscrew, proudly. "I am accustomed to appear at the bar."

"But you're crooked," retorted the King, "and that debars you. You may be a corking good lawyer, Mr. Popp, but I must ask you to with-draw your remarks."

"Very well," said the corkscrew, sadly; "I see I haven't any pull at this court."

"Permit me," continued the flatiron, "to press my suit, your Majesty. I do not wish to gloss over any fault the prisoner may have committed, if such a fault exists; but we owe her some con-sideration, and that's flat!"

"I'd like to hear from Prince Karver," said the King.

At this a stately carvingknife stepped forward and bowed.

"The Captain was wrong to bring this girl here, and she was wrong to come," he said. "But now that the foolish deed is done let us all prove our mettle and have a slashing good time."

"That's it! that's it!" screamed a fat chopping-knife. "We'll make mincemeat of the girl and hash of the chicken and sausage of the dog!"

There was a shout of approval at this and the King had to rap again for order.

"Gentlemen, gentlemen!" he said, "your remarks are somewhat cutting and rather disjointed, as might be expected from such acute intellects. But you give no reasons for your demands."

"See here, Kleaver; you make me tired," exclaimed a saucepan, strutting before the King very impudently. "You're about the worst King that ever reigned in Utensia, and that's saying a good deal. Why don't you run things yourself, instead of asking everybody's advice, like the big, clumsy idiot you are?"

The King sighed.

"I wish there wasn't a saucepan in my kingdom," he said. "You fellows are always stewing over something, and every once in a while you slop over and make a mess of it. Go hang yourself, sir—by the handle—and don't let me hear from you again."

Dorothy was much shocked by the dreadful language the utensils employed, and she thought that they must have had very little proper training. So she said, addressing the King, who seemed very unfit to rule his turbulent subjects:

"I wish you'd decide my fate right away. I can't stay here all day, trying to find out what you're going to do with me."

"This thing is becoming a regular broil, and it's time I took part in it," observed a big gridiron, coming forward.

"What I'd like to know," said a can-opener, in a shrill voice, "is why the girl came to our forest, anyhow, and why she intruded upon Captain Dipp—who ought to be called Dippy— and who she is, and where she came from, and where she is going, and why and wherefore and therefore and when."

"I'm sorry to see, Sir Jabber," remarked the King to the can-opener, "that you have such a prying disposition. As a matter of fact, all the things you mention are none of our business."

Having said this the King relighted his pipe, which had gone out.

"Tell me, please, what *is* our business?" inquired a potato-masher, winking at Dorothy somewhat impertinently. "I'm fond of little girls, myself, and it seems to me she has as much right to wander in the forest as we have."

"Who accuses the little girl, anyway?" inquired a rolling-pin. "What has she done?"

"I don't know," said the King. "What has she done, Captain Dipp?"

"That's the trouble, your Majesty. She hasn't done anything," replied the Captain.

"What do you want me to do?" asked Dorothy.

This question seemed to puzzle them all. Finally a chafingdish exclaimed, irritably:

"If no one can throw any light on this subject you must excuse me if I go out."

At this a big kitchen fork pricked up its ears and said in a tiny voice:

"Let's hear from Judge Sifter."

"That's proper," returned the King.

So Judge Sifter turned around slowly several times and then said:

"We have nothing against the girl except the stove-hearth upon which she sits. Therefore I order her instantly discharged."

"Discharged!" cried Dorothy. "Why, I never was discharged in my life, and I don't intend to be. If it's all the same to you, I'll resign."

"It's all the same," declared the King. "You are free—you and your companions—and may go wherever you like."

"Thank you," said the little girl. "But haven't you anything to eat in your kingdom? I'm hungry."

"Go into the woods and pick blackberries," advised the King, lying down upon his back again and preparing to go to sleep. "There isn't a morsel to eat in all Utensia, that I know of."

So Dorothy jumped up and said:

"Come on, Toto and Billina. If we can't find the camp we may find some blackberries."

The utensils drew back and allowed them to pass without protest, although Captain Dipp marched the Spoon Brigade in close order after them until they had reached the edge of the clearing.

There the spoons halted; but Dorothy and her companions entered the forest again and began searching diligently for a way back to the camp, that they might rejoin their party.

ING KI.FAVER

How THEY CAME TO BUNBURY

CHAPTER SEVENTEEN

WANDERING through the woods, without knowing where you are going or what adventure you are about to meet next, is not as pleasant as one might think. The woods are always beautiful and impressive, and if you are not worried or hungry you may enjoy them immensely; but Dorothy was worried and hungry that morning, so she paid little attention to the beauties of the forest, and hurried along as fast as she could go. She tried to keep in one direction and not circle around, but she was not at all sure that the direction she had chosen would lead her to the camp.

By and by, to her great joy, she came upon a path. It ran to the right and to the left, being lost in the trees in both directions, and just before her, upon a big oak, were fastened two

178

signs, with arms pointing both ways. One sign read:

☞ TAKE THE OTHER ROAD TO
BUNBURY

and the second sign read:

☞ TAKE THE OTHER ROAD TO
BUNNYBURY

"Well!" exclaimed Billina, eyeing the signs, "this looks as if we were getting back to civilization again."

"I'm not sure about the civil'zation, dear," replied the little girl; "but it looks as if we might get *somewhere,* and that's a big relief, anyhow."

"Which path shall we take?" inquired the Yellow Hen.

Dorothy stared at the signs thoughtfully.

"Bunbury sounds like something to eat," she said. "Let's go there."

"It's all the same to me," replied Billina. She had picked up enough bugs and insects from the moss as she went along to satisfy her own hunger, but the hen knew Dorothy could not eat bugs; nor could Toto.

The path to Bunbury seemed little traveled, but it was distinct enough and ran through the trees in a zigzag course until it finally led them to an open space filled with the queerest houses Dorothy had ever seen. They were all made of crackers, laid out in tiny squares, and were of many pretty and ornamental shapes, having balconies and porches with posts of bread-sticks and roofs shingled with wafer-crackers.

There were walks of bread-crusts leading from house to house and forming streets, and the place seemed to have many inhabitants.

When Dorothy, followed by Billina and Toto, entered the place, they found people walking the streets or assembled in groups talking together, or sitting upon the porches and balconies.

And what funny people they were!

Men, women and children were all made of buns and bread. Some were thin and others fat; some were white, some light brown and some very dark of complexion. A few of the buns, which seemed to form the more important class of the people, were neatly frosted. Some had raisins for eyes and currant buttons on their clothes; others had eyes of cloves and legs of stick cinnamon, and many wore hats and bonnets frosted pink and green.

There was something of a commotion in Bunbury when the strangers suddenly appeared among them. Women caught up their children and hurried into their houses, shutting the cracker doors carefully behind them. Some men ran so hastily that they tumbled over one another, while others, more brave, assembled in a group and faced the intruders defiantly.

Dorothy at once realized that she must act with caution in order not to frighten these shy people, who were evidently unused to the presence of strangers. There was a delightful fragrant odor of fresh bread in the town, and this made the little girl more hungry than ever. She told Toto and Billina to stay back while she slowly advanced toward the group that stood silently awaiting her.

"You must 'scuse me for coming unexpected," she said, softly, "but I really didn't know I was coming here until I arrived. I was lost in the woods, you know, and I'm as hungry as anything."

"Hungry!" they murmured, in a horrified chorus.

"Yes; I haven't had anything to eat since last night's supper," she explained. "Are there any eatables in Bunbury?"

They looked at one another undecidedly, and then one portly bun man, who seemed a person of consequence, stepped forward and said:

"Little girl, to be frank with you, we are all eatables. Everything in Bunbury is eatable to ravenous human creatures like you. But it is to escape being eaten and destroyed that we have secluded ourselves in this out-of-the-way place, and there is neither right nor justice in your coming here to feed upon us."

Dorothy looked at him longingly.

"You're bread, aren't you?" she asked.

"Yes; bread and butter. The butter is inside me, so it won't melt and run. I do the running myself."

At this joke all the others burst into a chorus of laughter, and Dorothy thought they couldn't be much afraid if they could laugh like that.

"Couldn't I eat something besides people?" she asked. "Couldn't I eat just one house, or a side-walk, or something? I wouldn't mind much what it was, you know."

"This is not a public bakery, child," replied the man, sternly. "It's private property."

"I know Mr.—Mr.—"

"My name is C. Bunn, Esquire," said the man. "C stands for Cinnamon, and this place is called after my family, which is the most aristocratic in the town."

"Oh, I don't know about that," objected another of the queer people. "The Grahams and the Browns and Whites are all excellent families, and there are none better of their kind. I'm a Boston Brown, myself."

"I admit you are all desirable citizens," said Mr. Bunn, rather stiffly; "but the fact remains that our town is called Bunbury."

"'Scuse me," interrupted Dorothy; "but I'm getting hungrier every minute. Now, if you're polite and kind, as I'm sure you ought to be, you'll let me eat *something*. There's so much to eat here that you never will miss it."

Then a big, puffed-up man, of a delicate brown color, stepped forward and said:

"I think it would be a shame to send this child away hungry, especially as she agrees to eat whatever we can spare and not touch our people."

"So do I, Pop," replied a Roll who stood near.

"What, then, do you suggest, Mr. Over?" inquired Mr. Bunn.

"Why, I'll let her eat my back fence, if she wants to. It's made of waffles, and they're very crisp and nice."

"She may also eat my wheelbarrow," added a pleasant looking Muffin. "It's made of nabiscos with a zuzu wheel."

"Very good; very good," remarked Mr. Bunn. "That is certainly very kind of you. Go with Pop Over and Mr. Muffin, little girl, and they will feed you."

"Thank you very much," said Dorothy, gratefully. "May I bring my dog Toto, and the Yellow Hen? They're hungry, too."

"Will you make them behave?" asked the Muffin.

"Of course," promised Dorothy.

"Then come along," said Pop Over.

So Dorothy and Billina and Toto walked up the street and the people seemed no longer to be at all afraid of them. Mr. Muffin's house came first, and as his wheelbarrow stood in the front yard the little girl ate that first. It didn't seem very fresh, but she was so hungry that she was not particular. Toto ate some, too, while Billina picked up the crumbs.

While the strangers were engaged in eating, many of the people came and stood in the street curiously watching them. Dorothy noticed six roguish looking brown children standing all in a row, and she asked:

"Who are you, little ones?"

"We're the Graham Gems," replied one; "and we're all twins."

"I wonder if your mother could spare one or two of you?" asked Billina, who decided that they were fresh baked; but at this dangerous question the six little gems ran away as fast as they could go.

"You mustn't say such things, Billina," said

Dorothy, reprovingly. "Now let's go into Pop Over's back yard and get the waffles."

"I sort of hate to let that fence go," remarked Mr. Over, nervously, as they walked toward his house. "The neighbors back of us are Soda Biscuits, and I don't care to mix with them."

"But I'm hungry yet," declared the girl. "That wheelbarrow wasn't very big."

"I've got a shortcake piano, but none of my family can play on it," he said, reflectively. "Suppose you eat that."

"All right," said Dorothy; "I don't mind. Anything to be accommodating."

So Mr. Over led her into the house, where she ate the piano, which was of an excellent flavor.

"Is there anything to drink here?" she asked.

"Yes; I've a milk pump and a water pump; which will you have?" he asked.

"I guess I'll try 'em both," said Dorothy.

So Mr. Over called to his wife, who brought into the yard a pail made of some kind of baked dough, and Dorothy pumped the pail full of cool, sweet milk and drank it eagerly.

The wife of Pop Over was several shades darker than her husband.

"Aren't you overdone?" the little girl asked her.

"No indeed," answered the woman. "I'm neither overdone nor done over; I'm just Mrs. Over, and I'm the President of the Bunbury Breakfast Band."

Dorothy thanked them for their hospitality and went away. At the gate Mr. Cinnamon Bunn met her and said he would show her around the town.

"We have some very interesting inhabitants," he remarked, walking stiffly beside her on his stick-cinnamon legs; "and all of us who are in good health are well bred. If you are no longer hungry we will call upon a few of the most important citizens."

Toto and Billina followed behind them, behaving very well, and a little way down the street they came to a handsome residence where Aunt Sally Lunn lived. The old lady was glad to meet the little girl and gave her a slice of white bread and butter which had been used as a door-mat. It was almost fresh and tasted better than anything Dorothy had eaten in the town.

"Where do you get the butter?" she inquired.

"We dig it out of the ground, which, as you may have observed, is all flour and meal," replied Mr. Bunn. "There is a butter mine just at the opposite side of the village. The trees which you see here are all doughleanders and doughderas, and in the season we get quite a crop of dough-nuts off them."

"I should think the flour would blow around and get into your eyes," said Dorothy.

"No," said he; "we are bothered with cracker dust sometimes, but never with flour."

Then he took her to see Johnny Cake, a cheerful old gentleman who lived near by.

"I suppose you've heard of me," said old Johnny, with an air of pride. "I'm a great favorite all over the world."

"Aren't you rather yellow?" asked Dorothy, looking at him critically.

"Maybe, child. But don't think I'm bilious, for I was never in better health in my life," replied the old gentleman. "If anything ailed me, I'd willingly acknowledge the corn."

"Johnny's a trifle stale," said Mr. Bunn, as they went away; "but he's a good mixer and never gets cross-grained. I will now take you to call upon some of my own relatives."

They visited the Sugar Bunns, the Currant Bunns and the Spanish Bunns, the latter having a decidedly foreign appearance. Then they saw the French Rolls, who were very polite to them, and made a brief call upon the Parker H. Rolls, who seemed a bit proud and overbearing.

"But they're not as stuck up as the Frosted Jumbles," declared Mr. Bunn, "who are people I really can't abide. I don't like to be suspicious or talk scandal, but sometimes I think the Jumbles have too much baking powder in them."

Just then a dreadful scream was heard, and Dorothy turned hastily around to find a scene of great excitement a little way down the street. The people were crowding around Toto and throwing at him everything they could find at hand. They pelted the little dog with hard-tack, crackers, and even articles of furniture which were hard baked and heavy enough for missiles.

Toto howled a little as the assortment of bake stuff struck him; but he stood still, with head bowed and tail between his legs, until Dorothy ran up and inquired what the matter was.

"Matter!" cried a rye loafer, indignantly, "why the horrid beast has eaten three of our dear Crumpets, and is now devouring a Salt-rising Biscuit!"

"Oh, Toto! How could you?" exclaimed Dorothy, much distressed.

Toto's mouth was full of his salt-rising victim; so he only whined and wagged his tail. But Billina, who had flown to the top of a cracker house to be in a safe place, called out:

"Don't blame him, Dorothy; the Crumpets dared him to do it."

"Yes, and you pecked out the eyes of a Raisin Bunn—one of our best citizens!" shouted a bread pudding, shaking its fist at the Yellow Hen.

"What's that! What's that?" wailed Mr. Cinnamon Bunn, who had now joined them. "Oh, what a misfortune—what a terrible misfortune!"

"See here," said Dorothy, determined to defend her pets, "I think we've treated you all pretty well, seeing you're eatables, an' reg'lar food for us. I've been kind to you, and eaten your old wheelbarrows and pianos and rubbish, an' not said a word. But Toto and Billina can't be 'spected to go hungry when the town's full of good things they like to eat, 'cause they can't understand your stingy ways as I do."

"You must leave here at once!" said Mr. Bunn, sternly.

"Suppose we won't go?" asked Dorothy, who was now much provoked.

"Then," said he, "we will put you into the great ovens where we are made, and bake you."

189

Dorothy gazed around and saw threatening looks upon the faces of all. She had not noticed any ovens in the town, but they might be there, nevertheless, for some of the inhabitants seemed very fresh. So she decided to go, and calling to Toto and Billina to follow her she marched up the street with as much dignity as possible, considering that she was followed by the hoots and cries of the buns and biscuits and other bake stuff.

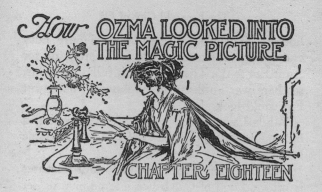

How OZMA LOOKED INTO THE MAGIC PICTURE

CHAPTER EIGHTEEN

PRINCESS Ozma was a very busy little ruler, for she looked carefully after the comfort and welfare of her people and tried to make them happy. If any quarrels arose she decided them justly; if any one needed counsel or advice she was ready and willing to listen to them.

For a day or two after Dorothy and her companions had started on their trip, Ozma was occupied with the affairs of her kingdom. Then she began to think of some manner of occupation for Uncle Henry and Aunt Em that would be light and easy and yet give the old people something to do.

She soon decided to make Uncle Henry the Keeper of the Jewels, for some one really was needed to count and look after the bins and barrels of emeralds, diamonds, rubies and other precious stones that were in the Royal Storehouses. That would keep Uncle Henry busy enough, but it was harder to find something for Aunt Em to do. The palace was full of servants, so there was no detail of housework that Aunt Em could look after.

While Ozma sat in her pretty room engaged in thought she happened to glance at her Magic Picture.

This was one of the most important treasures in all the Land of Oz. It was a large picture, set in a beautiful gold frame, and it hung in a prominent place upon a wall of Ozma's private room.

Usually this picture seemed merely a country scene, but whenever Ozma looked at it and wished to know what any of her friends or acquaintances were doing, the magic of this wonderful picture was straightway disclosed. For the country scene would gradually fade away and in its place would appear the likeness of the person or persons Ozma might wish to see, surrounded by the actual scenes in which they were then placed. In this way the Princess could view any part of the world she wished, and watch the actions of any one in whom she was interested.

Ozma had often seen Dorothy in her Kansas home by this means, and now, having a little leisure, she expressed a desire to see her little friend again. It was while the travelers were at Fuddlcumjig, and Ozma laughed merrily as she watched in the picture her friends trying to match the pieces of Grandmother Gnit.

"They seem happy and are doubtless having a good time," the girl Ruler said to herself; and then she began to think of the many adventures she herself had encountered with Dorothy.

The images of her friends now faded from the Magic Picture and the old landscape slowly reappeared.

Ozma was thinking of the time when with Dorothy and her army she marched to the Nome King's underground cavern, beyond the Land of Ev, and forced the old monarch to liberate his captives, who belonged to the Royal Family of Ev. That was the time when the Scarecrow nearly frightened the Nome King into fits by throwing one of Billina's eggs at him, and Dorothy had captured King Roquat's Magic Belt and brought it away with her to the Land of Oz.

The pretty Princess smiled at the recollection of this adventure, and then she wondered what had become of the Nome King since then. Merely because she was curious and had nothing better to do, Ozma glanced at the Magic Picture and wished to see in it the King of the Nomes.

Roquat the Red went every day into his tun-

nel to see how the work was getting along and
to hurry his workmen as much as possible. He
was there now, and Ozma saw him plainly in
the Magic Picture.

She saw the underground tunnel, reaching far
underneath the Deadly Desert which separated
the Land of Oz from the mountains beneath
which the Nome King had his extensive caverns.
She saw that the tunnel was being made in the
direction of the Emerald City, and knew at once
it was being dug so that the army of Nomes
could march through it and attack her own
beautiful and peaceful country.

"I suppose King Roquat is planning revenge
against us," she said, musingly, "and thinks he
can surprise us and make us his captives and
slaves. How sad it is that any one can have such
wicked thoughts! But I must not blame King
Roquat too severely, for he is a Nome, and his
nature is not so gentle as my own."

Then she dismissed from her mind further
thought of the tunnel, for that time, and began
to wonder if Aunt Em would not be happy as
Royal Mender of the Stockings of the Ruler of
Oz. Ozma wore few holes in her stockings; still,
they sometimes needed mending. Aunt Em
ought to be able to do that very nicely.

Next day the Princess watched the tunnel
again in her Magic Picture, and every day after-

ward she devoted a few minutes to inspecting the work. It was not especially interesting, but she felt that it was her duty.

Slowly but surely the big arched hole crept through the rocks underneath the deadly desert, and day by day it drew nearer and nearer to the Emerald City.

CHAPTER NINETEEN

DOROTHY left Bunbury the same way she had entered it and when they were in the forest again she said to Billina:

"I never thought that things good to eat could be so dis'gree'ble."

"Often I've eaten things that tasted good but were disagreeable afterward," returned the Yellow Hen. "I think, Dorothy, if eatables are going to act badly, it's better before than after you eat them."

"P'raps you're right," said the little girl, with a sigh. "But what shall we do now?"

"Let us follow the path back to the signpost," suggested Billina. "That will be better than getting lost again."

"Why, we're lost anyhow," declared Dorothy; "but I guess you're right about going back to that signpost, Billina."

They returned along the path to the place where they had first found it, and at once took "the other road" to Bunnybury. This road was a mere narrow strip, worn hard and smooth but not wide enough for Dorothy's feet to tread. Still it was a guide, and the walking through the forest was not at all difficult.

Before long they reached a high wall of solid white marble, and the path came to an end at this wall.

At first Dorothy thought there was no opening at all in the marble, but on looking closely she discovered a small square door about on a level with her head, and underneath this closed door was a bell-push. Near the bell-push a sign was painted in neat letters upon the marble, and the sign read:

No Admittance
Except on Business

This did not discourage Dorothy, however, and she rang the bell.

Pretty soon a bolt was cautiously withdrawn and the marble door swung slowly open. Then she saw it was not really a door, but a window, for several brass bars were placed across it, being set fast in the marble and so close together that the little girl's fingers might barely go between them. Back of the bars appeared the face of a white rabbit—a very sober and sedate face—with an eye-glass held in his left eye and attached to a cord in his button-hole.

"Well! what is it?" asked the rabbit, sharply.

"I'm Dorothy," said the girl, "and I'm lost, and—"

"State your business, please," interrupted the rabbit.

"My business," she replied, "is to find out where I am, and to—"

"No one is allowed in Bunnybury without an order or a letter of introduction from either Ozma of Oz or Glinda the Good," announced the rabbit; "so that that settles the matter," and he started to close the window.

"Wait a minute!" cried Dorothy. "I've got a letter from Ozma."

"From the Ruler of Oz?" asked the rabbit, doubtingly.

"Of course. Ozma's my best friend, you know; and I'm a Princess myself," she announced, earnestly.

"Hum—ha! Let me see your letter," returned the rabbit, as if he still doubted her.

So she hunted in her pocket and found the letter Ozma had given her. Then she handed it through the bars to the rabbit, who took it in his paws and opened it. He read it aloud in a pompous voice, as if to let Dorothy and Billina see that he was educated and could read writing. The letter was as follows:

"It will please me to have my subjects greet Princess Dorothy, the bearer of this royal missive, with the same courtesy and consideration they would extend to me."

"Ha—hum! It is signed 'Ozma of Oz,'" continued the rabbit, "and is sealed with the Great Seal of the Emerald City. Well, well, well! How strange! How remarkable!"

"What are you going to do about it?" inquired Dorothy, impatiently.

"We must obey the royal mandate," replied the rabbit. "We are subjects of Ozma of Oz, and we live in her country. Also we are under the protection of the great Sorceress Glinda the Good, who made us promise to respect Ozma's commands."

"Then may I come in?" she asked.

"I'll open the door," said the rabbit. He shut the window and disappeared, but a moment afterward a big door in the wall opened and admitted Dorothy to a small room, which seemed to be a part of the wall and built into it.

Here stood the rabbit she had been talking with, and now that she could see all of him she gazed at the creature in surprise. He was a good sized white rabbit with pink eyes, much like all other white rabbits. But the astonishing thing about him was the manner in which he was dressed. He wore a white satin jacket embroidered with gold, and having diamond buttons. His vest was rose-colored satin, with tourmaline buttons. His trousers were white, to correspond with the jacket, and they were baggy at the knees—like those of a zouave—being tied with knots of rose ribbons. His shoes were of white plush with diamond buckles, and his stockings were rose silk.

The richness and even magnificence of the rabbit's clothing made Dorothy stare at the little creature wonderingly. Toto and Billina had followed her into the room and when he saw them the rabbit ran to a table and sprang upon it nimbly. Then he looked at the three through his monocle and said:

"These companions, Princess, cannot enter Bunnybury with you."

"Why not?" asked Dorothy.

"In the first place they would frighten our people, who dislike dogs above all things on earth; and, secondly, the letter of the Royal Ozma does not mention them."

"But they're my friends," persisted Dorothy, "and go wherever I go."

"Not this time," said the rabbit, decidedly.

"You, yourself, Princess, are a welcome visitor, since you come so highly recommended; but unless you consent to leave the dog and the hen in this room I cannot permit you to enter the town."

"Never mind us, Dorothy," said Billina. "Go inside and see what the place is like. You can tell us about it afterward, and Toto and I will rest comfortably here until you return."

This seemed the best thing to do, for Dorothy was curious to see how the rabbit people lived and she was aware of the fact that her friends might frighten the timid little creatures. She had not forgotten how Toto and Billina had misbehaved in Bunbury, and perhaps the rabbit was wise to insist on their staying outside the town.

"Very well," she said, "I'll go in alone. I s'pose you're the King of this town, aren't you?"

"No," answered the rabbit, "I'm merely the Keeper of the Wicket, and a person of little importance, although I try to do my duty. I must now inform you, Princess, that before you enter our town you must consent to reduce."

"Reduce what?" asked Dorothy.

"Your size. You must become the size of the rabbits, although you may retain your own form."

"Wouldn't my clothes be too big for me?" she inquired.

"No; they will reduce when your body does."

"Can *you* make me smaller?" asked the girl.

"Easily," returned the rabbit.

"And will you make me big again, when I'm ready to go away?"

"I will," said he.

"All right, then; I'm willing," she announced.

The rabbit jumped from the table and ran—or rather hopped—to the further wall, where he opened a door so tiny that even Toto could scarcely have crawled through it.

"Follow me," he said.

Now, almost any other little girl would have declared that she could not get through so small a door; but Dorothy had already encountered so many fairy adventures that she believed nothing was impossible in the Land of Oz. So she quietly walked toward the door, and at every step she grew smaller and smaller until, by the time the opening was reached, she could pass through it with ease. Indeed, as she stood beside the rabbit, who sat upon his hind legs and used his paws as hands, her head was just about as high as his own.

Then the Keeper of the Wicket passed through and she followed, after which the door swung shut and locked itself with a sharp click.

Dorothy now found herself in a city so strange and beautiful that she gave a gasp of surprise.

The high marble wall extended all around the place and shut out all the rest of the world. And here were marble houses of curious forms, most of them resembling overturned kettles but with delicate slender spires and minarets running far up into the sky. The streets were paved with white marble and in front of each house was a lawn of rich green clover. Everything was

as neat as wax, the green and white contrasting prettily together.

But the rabbit people were, after all, the most amazing things Dorothy saw. The streets were full of them, and their costumes were so splendid that the rich dress of the Keeper of the Wicket was commonplace when compared with the others. Silks and satins of delicate hues seemed always used for material, and nearly every costume sparkled with exquisite gems.

But the lady rabbits outshone the gentlemen rabbits in splendor, and the cut of their gowns was really wonderful. They wore bonnets, too, with feathers and jewels in them, and some wheeled baby carriages in which the girl could see wee bunnies. Some were lying asleep while others lay sucking their paws and looking around them with big pink eyes.

As Dorothy was no bigger in size than the grown-up rabbits she had a chance to observe them closely before they noticed her presence. Then they did not seem at all alarmed, although the little girl naturally became the center of attraction and all regarded her with great curiosity.

"Make way!" cried the Keeper of the Wicket, in a pompous voice; "make way for Princess Dorothy, who comes from Ozma of Oz."

Hearing this announcement, the throng of rabbits gave place to them on the walks, and as Dorothy passed along they all bowed their heads respectfully.

Walking thus through several handsome streets they came to a square in the center of the City. In this square were some pretty trees and a statue in bronze of Glinda the Good, while beyond it were the portals of the Royal Palace— an extensive and imposing building of white marble covered with a filigree of frosted gold.

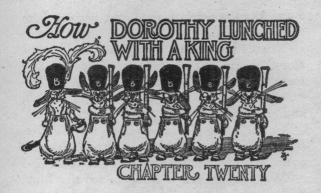

HOW DOROTHY LUNCHED WITH A KING

CHAPTER TWENTY

A LINE of rabbit soldiers was drawn up before the palace entrance, and they wore green and gold uniforms with high shakos upon their heads and held tiny spears in their hands. The Captain had a sword and a white plume in his shako.

"Salute!" cried the Keeper of the Wicket. "Salute Princess Dorothy, who comes from Ozma of Oz!"

"Salute!" yelled the Captain, and all the soldiers promptly saluted.

They now entered the great hall of the palace, where they met a gaily dressed attendant, from whom the Keeper of the Wicket inquired if the King were at leisure.

"I think so," was the reply. "I heard his Majesty blubbering and wailing as usual only a few minutes ago. If he doesn't stop acting like a cry-baby I'm going to resign my position here and go to work."

"What's the matter with your King?" asked Dorothy, surprised to hear the rabbit attendant speak so disrespectfully of his monarch.

"Oh, he doesn't want to be King, that's all; and he simply *has* to," was the reply.

"Come!" said the Keeper of the Wicket, sternly; "lead us to his Majesty; and do not air our troubles before strangers, I beg of you."

"Why, if this girl is going to see the King, he'll air his own troubles," returned the attendant.

"That is his royal privilege," declared the Keeper.

So the attendant led them into a room all draped with cloth-of-gold and furnished with satin-covered gold furniture. There was a throne in this room, set on a dais and having a big cushioned seat, and on this seat reclined the Rabbit King. He was lying on his back, with his paws in the air, and whining very like a puppy-dog.

"Your Majesty! your Majesty! Get up. Here's a visitor," called out the attendant.

The King rolled over and looked at Dorothy with one watery pink eye. Then he sat up and wiped his eyes carefully with a silk handkerchief and put on his jeweled crown, which had fallen off.

"Excuse my grief, fair stranger," he said, in a sad voice. "You behold in me the most miserable monarch in all the world. What time is it, Blinkem?"

"One o'clock, your Majesty," replied the attendant to whom the question was addressed.

"Serve luncheon at once!" commanded the King. "Luncheon for two—that's for my visitor and me—and see that the human has some sort of food she's accustomed to."

"Yes, your Majesty," answered the attendant, and went away.

"Tie my shoe, Bristle," said the King to the Keeper of the Wicket. "Ah, me! how unhappy I am!"

"What seems to be worrying your Majesty?" asked Dorothy.

"Why, it's this king business, of course," he returned, while the Keeper tied his shoe. "I didn't want to be King of Bunnybury at all, and the rabbits all knew it. So they elected me—to save themselves from such a dreadful fate, I suppose—and here I am, shut up in a palace, when I might be free and happy."

"Seems to me," said Dorothy, "it's a great thing to be a King."

"Were you ever a King?" inquired the monarch.

"No," she answered, laughing.

"Then you know nothing about it," he said. "I haven't inquired who you are, but it doesn't matter. While we're at luncheon, I'll tell you all my troubles. They're a great deal more interesting than anything you can say about yourself."

"Perhaps they are, to you," replied Dorothy.

"Luncheon is served!" cried Blinkem, throwing open the door, and in came a dozen rabbits in livery, all bearing trays which they placed upon the table, where they arranged the dishes in an orderly manner.

"Now clear out—all of you!" exclaimed the King. "Bristle, you may wait outside, in case I want you."

When they had gone and the King was alone with Dorothy he came down from his throne, tossed his crown into a corner and kicked his ermine robe under the table.

"Sit down," he said, "and try to be happy. It's useless for me to try, because I'm always wretched and miserable. But I'm hungry, and I hope you are."

"I am," said Dorothy. "I've only eaten a wheelbarrow and a piano to-day—oh, yes! and a

slice of bread and butter that used to be a door-mat."

"That sounds like a square meal," remarked the King, seating himself opposite her; "but perhaps it wasn't a square piano. Eh?"

Dorothy laughed.

"You don't seem so very unhappy now," she said.

"But I am," protested the King, fresh tears gathering in his eyes. "Even my jokes are miserable. I'm wretched, woeful, afflicted, distressed and dismal as an individual can be. Are you not sorry for me?"

"No," answered Dorothy, honestly, "I can't say I am. Seems to me that for a rabbit you're right in clover. This is the prettiest little city I ever saw."

"Oh, the city is good enough," he admitted. "Glinda, the Good Sorceress, made it for us because she was fond of rabbits. I don't mind the City so much, although I wouldn't live here if I had my choice. It is being King that has absolutely ruined my happiness."

"Why wouldn't you live here by choice?" she asked.

"Because it is all unnatural, my dear. Rabbits are out of place in such luxury. When I was young I lived in a burrow in the forest. I was surrounded by enemies and often had to run for my life. It was hard getting enough to eat, at times, and when I found a bunch of clover I had to listen and look for danger while I ate it. Wolves prowled around the hole in which I lived and sometimes I didn't dare stir out for days at a time. Oh, how happy and contented I was then! I was a real rabbit, as nature made me—wild and free!—and I even enjoyed listening to the startled throbbing of my own heart!"

"I've often thought," said Dorothy, who was busily eating, "that it would be fun to be a rabbit."

"It *is* fun—when you're the genuine article," agreed his Majesty. "But look at me now! I live in a marble palace instead of a hole in the ground. I have all I want to eat, without the joy of hunting for it. Every day I must dress in fine clothes and wear that horrible crown till it makes my head ache. Rabbits come to me with all sorts of troubles, when my own troubles are the only ones I care about. When I walk out I can't hop and run; I must strut on my rear legs and wear an ermine robe! And the soldiers salute me and the band plays and the other rabbits laugh and clap their paws and cry out: 'Hail to the King!' Now let me ask you, as a friend and a young lady of good judgment: isn't all this pomp and foolishness enough to make a decent rabbit miserable?"

"Once," said Dorothy, reflectively, "men were wild and unclothed and lived in caves and hunted for food as wild beasts do. But they got civ'lized, in time, and now they'd hate to go back to the old days."

"That is an entirely different case," replied the King. "None of you Humans were civilized in one lifetime. It came to you by degrees. But I have known the forest and the free life, and that is why I resent being civilized all at once, against my will, and being made a King with a crown and an ermine robe. Pah!"

"If you don't like it, why don't you resign?" she asked.

"Impossible!" wailed the Rabbit, wiping his eyes again with his handkerchief. "There's a beastly law in this town that forbids it. When one is elected a King there's no getting out of it."

"Who made the laws?" inquired Dorothy.

"The same Sorceress who made the town— Glinda the Good. She built the wall, and fixed up the City, and gave us several valuable enchantments, and made the laws. Then she invited all the pink-eyed white rabbits of the forest to come here, after which she left us to our fate."

"What made you 'cept the invitation, and come here?" asked the child.

"I didn't know how dreadful city life was,

and I'd no idea I would be elected King," said he, sobbing bitterly. "And—and—now I'm It— with a capital I—and can't escape!"

"I know Glinda," remarked Dorothy, eating for dessert a dish of charlotte russe, "and when I see her again I'll ask her to put another King in your place."

"Will you? Will you, indeed?" asked the King, joyfully.

"I will if you want me to," she replied.

"Hurroo—hurray!" shouted the King; and then he jumped up from the table and danced wildly about the room, waving his napkin like a flag and laughing with glee.

After a time he managed to control his delight and returned to the table.

"When are you likely to see Glinda?" he inquired.

"Oh, p'raps in a few days," said Dorothy.

"And you won't forget to ask her?"

"Of course not."

"Princess," said the Rabbit King, earnestly, "you have relieved me of a great unhappiness, and I am very grateful. Therefore I propose to entertain you, since you are my guest and I am the King, as a slight mark of my appreciation. Come with me to my reception hall."

He then summoned Bristle and said to him:

"Assemble all the nobility in the great reception hall, and also tell Blinkem that I want him immediately."

The Keeper of the Wicket bowed and hurried away, and his Majesty turned to Dorothy and continued: "We'll have time for a walk in the gardens before the people get here."

The gardens were back of the palace and were filled with beautiful flowers and fragrant shrubs, with many shade and fruit trees and marble paved walks running in every direction. As they entered this place Blinkem came running to the King, who gave him several orders in a low voice. Then his Majesty rejoined Dorothy and led her through the gardens, which she admired very much.

"What lovely clothes your Majesty wears!" she said, glancing at the rich blue satin costume, embroidered with pearls, in which the King was dressed.

"Yes," he returned, with an air of pride, "this is one of my favorite suits; but I have a good many that are even more elaborate. We have excellent tailors in Bunnybury, and Glinda supplies all the material. By the way, you might ask the Sorceress, when you see her, to permit me to keep my wardrobe."

"But if you go back to the forest you will not need clothes," she said.

"N—o!" he faltered; "that may be so. But I've dressed up so long that I'm used to it, and I don't imagine I'd care to run around naked again. So perhaps the Good Glinda will let me keep the costumes."

"I'll ask her," agreed Dorothy.

Then they left the gardens and went into a fine big reception hall, where rich rugs were spread upon the tiled floors and the furniture was exquisitely carved and studded with jewels. The King's chair was an especially pretty piece of furniture, being in the shape of a silver lily with one leaf bent over to form the seat. The silver was everywhere thickly encrusted with diamonds and the seat was upholstered in white satin.

"Oh, what a splendid chair!" cried Dorothy,

clasping her hands admiringly.

"Isn't it?" answered the King, proudly. "It is my favorite seat, and I think it especially becoming to my complexion. While I think of it, I wish you'd ask Glinda to let me keep this lily chair when I go away."

"It wouldn't look very well in a hole in the ground, would it?" she suggested.

"Maybe not; but I'm used to sitting in it and I'd like to take it with me," he answered. "But here come the ladies and gentlemen of the court; so please sit beside me and be presented."

How THE KING CHANGED HIS MIND

CHAPTER TWENTY-ONE

JUST then a rabbit band of nearly fifty pieces marched in, playing upon golden instruments and dressed in neat uniforms. Following the band came the nobility of Bunnybury, all richly dressed and hopping along on their rear legs. Both the ladies and the gentlemen wore white gloves upon their paws, with their rings on the outside of the gloves, as this seemed to be the fashion here. Some of the lady rabbits carried lorgnettes, while many of the gentlemen rabbits wore monocles in their left eyes.

The courtiers and their ladies paraded past the King, who introduced Princess Dorothy to each couple in a very graceful manner. Then the company seated themselves in chairs and on sofas and looked expectantly at their monarch.

"It is our royal duty, as well as our royal

pleasure," he said, "to provide fitting entertainment for our distinguished guest. We will now present the Royal Band of Whiskered Friskers."

As he spoke the musicians, who had arranged themselves in a corner, struck up a dance melody while into the room pranced the Whiskered Friskers. They were eight pretty rabbits dressed only in gauzy purple skirts fastened around their waists with diamond bands. Their whiskers were colored a rich purple, but otherwise they were pure white.

After bowing before the King and Dorothy the Friskers began their pranks, and these were so comical that Dorothy laughed with real enjoyment. They not only danced together, whirling and gyrating around the room, but they leaped over one another, stood upon their heads and hopped and skipped here and there so nimbly that it was hard work to keep track of them. Finally they all made double somersaults and turned handsprings out of the room.

The nobility enthusiastically applauded, and Dorothy applauded with them.

"They're fine!" she said to the King.

"Yes, the Whiskered Friskers are really very clever," he replied. "I shall hate to part with them when I go away, for they have often amused me when I was very miserable. I wonder if you would ask Glinda—"

"No, it wouldn't do at all," declared Dorothy, positively. "There wouldn't be room in your hole in the ground for so many rabbits, 'spec'ly when you get the lily chair and your clothes there. Don't think of such a thing, your Majesty."

The King sighed. Then he stood up and announced to the company:

"We will now behold a military drill by my picked Bodyguard of Royal Pikemen."

Now the band played a march and a company of rabbit soldiers came in. They wore green and gold uniforms and marched very stiffly but in perfect time. Their spears, or pikes, had slender shafts of polished silver with golden heads, and during the drill they handled these weapons with wonderful dexterity.

"I should think you'd feel pretty safe with such a fine Bodyguard," remarked Dorothy.

"I do," said the King. "They protect me from every harm. I suppose Glinda wouldn't—"

"No," interrupted the girl; "I'm sure she wouldn't. It's the King's own Bodyguard, and when you are no longer King you can't have 'em."

The King did not reply, but he looked rather sorrowful for a time.

When the soldiers had marched out he said to the company:

"The Royal Jugglers will now appear."

Dorothy had seen many jugglers in her lifetime, but never any so interesting as these. There were six of them, dressed in black satin embroidered with queer symbols in silver—a costume which contrasted strongly with their snow-white fur.

First they pushed in a big red ball and three of the rabbit jugglers stood upon its top and made it roll. Then two of them caught up a third and tossed him into the air, all vanishing, until only the two were left. Then one of these tossed the other upward and remained alone of all his fellows. This last juggler now touched the red ball, which fell apart, being hollow, and the five rabbits who had disappeared in the air scrambled out of the hollow ball.

Next they all clung together and rolled swiftly upon the floor. When they came to a stop only one fat rabbit juggler was seen, the others seeming to be inside him. This one leaped lightly into the air and when he came down he exploded and separated into the original six. Then four of them rolled themselves into round balls and the other two tossed them around and played ball with them.

These were but a few of the tricks the rabbit jugglers performed, and they were so skillful that all the nobility and even the King applauded as loudly as did Dorothy.

"I suppose there are no rabbit jugglers in all the world to compare with these," remarked the King. "And since I may not have the Whiskered Friskers or my Bodyguard, you might ask Glinda to let me take away just two or three of these jugglers. Will you?"

"I'll ask her," replied Dorothy, doubtfully.

"Thank you," said the King; "thank you very much. And now you shall listen to the Winsome Waggish Warblers, who have often cheered me in my moments of anguish."

The Winsome Waggish Warblers proved to be a quartette of rabbit singers, two gentlemen and two lady rabbits. The gentlemen Warblers wore full-dress swallow-tailed suits of white satin, with pearls for buttons, while the lady Warblers were gowned in white satin dresses with long trails.

The first song they sang began in this way:

"When a rabbit gets a habit
    Of living in a city
And wearing clothes and furbelows
    And jewels rare and pretty,
He scorns the Bun who has to run
    And burrow in the ground
And pities those whose watchful foes
    Are man and gun and hound."

Dorothy looked at the King when she heard this song and noticed that he seemed disturbed and ill at ease.

"I don't like that song," he said to the Warblers. "Give us something jolly and rollicking."

So they sang to a joyous, tinkling melody as follows:

"Bunnies gay
Delight to play
In their fairy town secure;
Ev'ry frisker
Flirts his whisker
At a pink-eyed girl demure.
Ev'ry maid
In silk arrayed
At her partner shyly glances,
Paws are grasped,
Waists are clasped
As they whirl in giddy dances.
Then together
Through the heather
'Neath the moonlight soft they stroll;
Each is very
Blithe and merry,
Gamboling with laughter droll.
Life is fun
To ev'ry one

Guarded by our magic charm
    For to dangers
    We are strangers,
Safe from any thought of harm."

"You see," said Dorothy to the King, when the song ended, "the rabbits all seem to like Bunnybury except you. And I guess you're the only one that ever has cried or was unhappy and wanted to get back to your muddy hole in the ground."

His Majesty seemed thoughtful, and while the servants passed around glasses of nectar and plates of frosted cakes their King was silent and a bit nervous.

When the refreshments had been enjoyed by all and the servants had retired Dorothy said:

"I must go now, for it's getting late and I'm lost. I've got to find the Wizard and Aunt Em and Uncle Henry and all the rest sometime before night comes, if I poss'bly can."

"Won't you stay with us?" asked the King. "You will be very welcome."

"No, thank you," she replied. "I must get back to my friends. And I want to see Glinda just as soon as I can, you know."

So the King dismissed his court and said he would himself walk with Dorothy to the gate. He did not weep nor groan any more, but his long face was quite solemn and his big ears hung dejectedly on each side of it. He still wore his crown and his ermine and walked with a handsome gold-headed cane.

When they arrived at the room in the wall the little girl found Toto and Billina waiting for her very patiently. They had been liberally fed by some of the attendants and were in no hurry to leave such comfortable quarters.

The Keeper of the Wicket was by this time back in his old place, but he kept a safe distance from Toto. Dorothy bade good bye to the King as they stood just inside the wall:

"You've been good to me," she said, "and I thank you ever so much. As soon as poss'ble I'll see Glinda and ask her to put another King in your place and send you back into the wild forest. And I'll ask her to let you keep some of your clothes and the lily chair and one or two jugglers to amuse you. I'm sure she will do it, 'cause she's so kind she doesn't like any one to be unhappy."

"Ahem!" said the King, looking rather downcast. "I don't like to trouble you with my misery; so you needn't see Glinda."

"Oh, yes I will," she replied. "It won't be any trouble at all."

"But, my dear," continued the King, in an embarrassed way, "I've been thinking the subject over carefully, and I find there are a lot of pleasant things here in Bunnybury that I would miss if I went away. So perhaps I'd better stay."

Dorothy laughed. Then she looked grave.

"It won't do for you to be a King and a cry-baby at the same time," she said. "You've been making all the other rabbits unhappy and discontented with your howls about being so miserable. So I guess it's better to have another King."

"Oh, no indeed!" exclaimed the King, earnestly. "If you won't say anything to Glinda I'll promise to be merry and gay all the time, and never cry or wail again."

"Honor bright?" she asked.

"On the royal word of a King I promise it!" he answered.

"All right," said Dorothy. "You'd be a reg'lar lunatic to want to leave Bunnybury for a wild life in the forest, and I'm sure any rabbit outside the city would be glad to take your place."

"Forget it, my dear; forget all my foolishness," pleaded the King, earnestly. "Hereafter I'll try to enjoy myself and do my duty by my subjects."

So then she left him and entered through the little door into the room in the wall, where she grew gradually bigger and bigger until she had resumed her natural size.

The Keeper of the Wicket let them out into the forest and told Dorothy that she had been of great service to Bunnybury because she had brought their dismal King to a realization of the pleasure of ruling so beautiful a city.

"I shall start a petition to have your statue erected beside Glinda's in the public square," said the Keeper. "I hope you will come again, some day, and see it."

"Perhaps I shall," she replied.

Then, followed by Toto and Billina, she walked away from the high marble wall and started back along the narrow path toward the sign-post.

How THE WIZARD FOUND DOROTHY

CHAPTER TWENTY-TWO

WHEN they came to the signpost, there, to their joy, were the tents of the Wizard pitched beside the path and the kettle bubbling merrily over a fire. The Shaggy Man and Omby Amby were gathering firewood while Uncle Henry and Aunt Em sat in their camp chairs talking with the Wizard.

They all ran forward to greet Dorothy, as she approached, and Aunt Em exclaimed: "Goodness gracious, child! Where have you been?"

"You've played hookey the whole day," added the Shaggy Man, reproachfully.

"Well, you see, I've been lost," explained the little girl, "and I've tried awful hard to find the way back to you, but just couldn't do it."

"Did you wander in the forest all day?" asked Uncle Henry.

"You must be a'most starved!" said Aunt Em.

"No," said Dorothy, "I'm not hungry. I had a wheelbarrow and a piano for breakfast, and lunched with a King."

"Ah!" exclaimed the Wizard, nodding with a bright smile. "So you've been having adventures again."

"She's stark crazy!" cried Aunt Em. "Whoever heard of eating a wheelbarrow?"

"It wasn't very big," said Dorothy; "and it had a zuzu wheel."

"And I ate the crumbs," added Billina, soberly.

"Sit down and tell us about it," begged the Wizard. "We've hunted for you all day, and at last I noticed your footsteps in this path—and the tracks of Billina. We found the path by accident, and seeing it only led to two places I decided you were at either one or the other of those places. So we made camp and waited for you to return. And now, Dorothy, tell us where you have been—to Bunbury or to Bunnybury?"

"Why, I've been to both," she replied; "but first I went to Utensia, which isn't on any path at all."

She then sat down and related the day's adventures, and you may be sure Aunt Em and Uncle Henry were much astonished at the story.

"But after seeing the Cuttenclips and the Fuddles," remarked her uncle, "we ought not to wonder at anything in this strange country."

"Seems like the only common and ordinary folks here are ourselves," rejoined Aunt Em, diffidently.

"Now that we're together again, and one re-united party," observed the Shaggy Man, "what are we to do next?"

"Have some supper and a night's rest," answered the Wizard promptly, "and then proceed upon our journey."

"Where to?" asked the Captain General.

"We haven't visited the Rigmaroles or the Flutterbudgets yet," said Dorothy. "I'd like to see them—wouldn't you?"

"They don't sound very interesting," objected Aunt Em. "But perhaps they are."

"And then," continued the little Wizard, "we will call upon the Tin Woodman and Jack Pumpkinhead and our old friend the Scarecrow, on our way home."

"That will be nice!" cried Dorothy, eagerly.

"Can't say *they* sound very interesting, either," remarked Aunt Em.

"Why, they're the best friends I have!" asserted the little girl, "and you're sure to like them, Aunt Em, 'cause *ever'*-body likes them."

By this time twilight was approaching, so they ate the fine supper which the Wizard magically produced from the kettle and then went to bed in the cosy tents.

They were all up bright and early next morning, but Dorothy didn't venture to wander from the camp again for fear of more accidents.

"Do you know where there's a road?" she asked the little man.

"No, my dear," replied the Wizard; "but I'll find one."

After breakfast he waved his hand toward the tents and they became handkerchiefs again, which were at once returned to the pockets of their owners. Then they all climbed into the red wagon and the Sawhorse inquired:

"Which way?"

"Never mind which way," replied the Wizard. "Just go as you please and you're sure to be right. I've enchanted the wheels of the wagon, and they will roll in the right direction, never fear."

As the Sawhorse started away through the trees Dorothy said:

"If we had one of those new-fashioned airships we could float away over the top of the forest, and look down and find just the places we want."

"Airship? Pah!" retorted the little man, scornfully. "I hate those things, Dorothy, although they are nothing new to either you or me. I was a balloonist for many years, and once my balloon carried me to the Land of Oz, and once to the

Vegetable Kingdom. And once Ozma had a Gump that flew all over this kingdom and had sense enough to go where it was told to—which airships won't do. The house which the cyclone brought to Oz all the way from Kansas, with you and Toto in it—was a real airship at the time; so you see we've had plenty of experience flying with the birds."

"Airships are not so bad, after all," declared Dorothy. "Some day they'll fly all over the world, and perhaps bring people even to the Land of Oz."

"I must speak to Ozma about that," said the Wizard, with a slight frown. "It wouldn't do at all, you know, for the Emerald City to become a way-station on an airship line."

"No," said Dorothy, "I don't s'pose it would. But what can we do to prevent it?"

"I'm working out a magic recipe to fuddle men's brains, so they'll never make an airship that will go where they want it to go," the Wizard confided to her. "That won't keep the things from flying, now and then, but it'll keep them from flying to the Land of Oz."

Just then the Sawhorse drew the wagon out of the forest and a beautiful landscape lay spread before the travelers' eyes. Moreover, right before them was a good road that wound away through the hills and valleys.

"Now," said the Wizard, with evident delight, "we are on the right track again, and there is nothing more to worry about."

"It's a foolish thing to take chances in a strange country," observed the Shaggy Man. "Had we kept to the roads we never would have been lost. Roads always lead to some place, else they wouldn't be roads."

"This road," added the Wizard, "leads to Rigmarole Town. I'm sure of that because I enchanted the wagon wheels."

Sure enough, after riding along the road for an hour or two they entered a pretty valley where a village was nestled among the hills. The houses were Munchkin shaped, for they were all domes, with windows wider than they were high, and pretty balconies over the front doors.

Aunt Em was greatly relieved to find this town "neither paper nor patch-work," and the only surprising thing about it was that it was so far distant from all other towns.

As the Sawhorse drew the wagon into the main street the travelers noticed that the place was filled with people, standing in groups and seeming to be engaged in earnest conversation. So occupied with themselves were the inhabitants that they scarcely noticed the strangers at all. So the Wizard stopped a boy and asked:

"Is this Rigmarole Town?"

"Sir," replied the boy, "if you have traveled very much you will have noticed that every town differs from every other town in one way or another and so by observing the methods of the people and the way they live as well as the style of their dwelling places it ought not to be a difficult thing to make up your mind without the trouble of asking questions whether the town bears the appearance of the one you intended to visit or whether perhaps having taken a different road from the one you should have taken you have made an error in your way and arrived at some point where—"

"Land sakes!" cried Aunt Em, impatiently; "what's all this rigmarole about?"

"That's it!" said the Wizard, laughing merrily. "It's a rigmarole because the boy is a Rigmarole and we've come to Rigmarole Town."

"Do they all talk like that?" asked Dorothy, wonderingly.

"He might have said 'yes' or 'no' and settled the question," observed Uncle Henry.

"Not here," said Omby Amby. "I don't believe the Rigmaroles know what 'yes' or 'no' means."

While the boy had been talking several other people had approached the wagon and listened intently to his speech. Then they began talking to one another in long, deliberate speeches, where many words were used but little was said. But when the strangers criticised them so frankly one of the women, who had no one else to talk to, began an address to them, saying:

"It is the easiest thing in the world for a person to say 'yes' or 'no' when a question that is asked for the purpose of gaining information or satisfying the curiosity of the one who has given expression to the inquiry has attracted the attention of an individual who may be competent either from personal experience or the experience of others to answer it with more or less correctness or at least an attempt to satisfy the desire for information on the part of the one who has made the inquiry by—"

"Dear me!" exclaimed Dorothy, interrupting the speech. "I've lost all track of what you are saying."

"Don't let her begin over again, for goodness sake!" cried Aunt Em.

But the woman did not begin again. She did not even stop talking, but went right on as she had begun, the words flowing from her mouth in a stream.

"I'm quite sure that if we waited long enough and listened carefully, some of these people might be able to tell us something, in time," said the Wizard.

"Don't let's wait," returned Dorothy. "I've heard of the Rigmaroles, and wondered what they were like; but now I know, and I'm ready to move on."

"So am I," declared Uncle Henry; "we're wasting time here."

"Why, we're all ready to go," added the Shaggy Man, putting his fingers to his ears to shut out the monotonous babble of those around the wagon.

So the Wizard spoke to the Sawhorse, who trotted nimbly through the village and soon gained the open country on the other side of it. Dorothy looked back, as they rode away, and noticed that the woman had not yet finished her speech but was talking as glibly as ever, although no one was near to hear her.

"If those people wrote books," Omby Amby remarked with a smile, "it would take a whole library to say the cow jumped over the moon."

"Perhaps some of 'em do write books," asserted the little Wizard. "I've read a few rigmaroles that might have come from this very town."

"Some of the college lecturers and ministers are certainly related to these people," observed the Shaggy Man; "and it seems to me the Land of Oz is a little ahead of the United States in some of its laws. For here, if one can't talk clearly, and straight to the point, they send him to Rigmarole Town; while Uncle Sam lets him roam around wild and free, to torture innocent people."

Dorothy was thoughtful. The Rigmaroles had

made a strong impression upon her. She decided that whenever she spoke, after this, she would use only enough words to express what she wanted to say.

How THEY ENCOUNTERED THE FLUTTERBUDGETS

CHAPTER TWENTY-THREE

THEY were soon among the pretty hills and valleys again, and the Sawhorse sped up hill and down at a fast and easy pace, the roads being hard and smooth. Mile after mile was speedily covered, and before the ride had grown at all tiresome they sighted another village. The place seemed even larger than Rigmarole Town, but was not so attractive in appearance.

"This must be Flutterbudget Center," declared the Wizard. "You see, it's no trouble at all to find places if you keep to the right road."

"What are the Flutterbudgets like?" inquired Dorothy.

"I do not know, my dear. But Ozma has given them a town all their own, and I've heard that whenever one of the people becomes a Flutterbudget he is sent to this place to live."

"That is true," Omby Amby added; "Flutterbudget Center and Rigmarole Town are called 'the Defensive Settlements of Oz.' "

The village they now approached was not built in a valley, but on top of a hill, and the road they followed wound around the hill like a corkscrew, ascending the hill easily until it came to the town.

"Look out!" screamed a voice. "Look out, or you'll run over my child!"

They gazed around and saw a woman standing upon the sidewalk nervously wringing her hands as she gazed at them appealingly.

"Where is your child?" asked the Sawhorse.

"In the house," said the woman, bursting into tears; "but if it should happen to be in the road, and you ran over it, those great wheels would crush my darling to jelly. Oh, dear! oh dear! Think of my darling child being crushed to jelly by those great wheels!"

"Gid-dap!" said the Wizard, sharply, and the Sawhorse started on.

They had not gone far before a man ran out of a house shouting wildly: "Help! Help!"

The Sawhorse stopped short and the Wizard and Uncle Henry and the Shaggy Man and Omby Amby jumped out of the wagon and ran to the poor man's assistance. Dorothy followed them as quickly as she could.

"What's the matter?" asked the Wizard.

"Help! help!" screamed the man; "my wife has cut her finger off and she's bleeding to death!"

Then he turned and rushed back to the house, and all the party went with him. They found a woman in the front dooryard moaning and groaning as if in great pain.

"Be brave, madam!" said the Wizard, consolingly. "You won't die just because you have cut off a finger, you may be sure."

"But I haven't cut off a finger!" she sobbed.

"Then what *has* happened?" asked Dorothy.

"I—I pricked my finger with a needle while I was sewing, and—and the blood came!" she replied. "And now I'll have blood-poisoning, and the doctors will cut off my finger, and that will give me a fever and I shall die!"

"Pshaw!" said Dorothy; "I've pricked my finger many a time, and nothing happened."

"Really?" asked the woman, brightening and wiping her eyes upon her apron.

"Why, it's nothing at all," declared the girl. "You're more scared than hurt."

"Ah, that's because she's a Flutterbudget," said the Wizard, nodding wisely. "I think I know now what these people are like."

"So do I," announced Dorothy.

"Oh, boo-hoo-hoo!" sobbed the woman, giving way to a fresh burst of grief.

"What's wrong now?" asked the Shaggy Man.

"Oh, suppose I had pricked my foot!" she wailed. "Then the doctors would have cut my foot off, and I'd be lamed for life!"

"Surely, ma'am," replied the Wizard, "and if you'd pricked your nose they might cut your head off. But you see you didn't."

"But I might have!" she exclaimed, and began to cry again. So they left her and drove away in their wagon. And her husband came out and began calling "Help!" as he had before; but no one seemed to pay any attention to him.

As the travelers turned into another street they found a man walking excitedly up and down the pavement. He appeared to be in a very nervous condition and the Wizard stopped him to ask:

"Is anything wrong, sir?"

"Everything is wrong," answered the man, dismally. "I can't sleep."

"Why not?" inquired Omby Amby.

"If I go to sleep I'll have to shut my eyes," he explained; "and if I shut my eyes they may grow together, and then I'd be blind for life!"

"Did you ever hear of any one's eyes growing together?" asked Dorothy.

"No," said the man, "I never did. But it would be a dreadful thing, wouldn't it? And the thought of it makes me so nervous I'm afraid to go to sleep."

"There's no help for this case," declared the Wizard; and they went on.

At the next street corner a woman rushed up to them crying:

"Save my baby! Oh, good, kind people, save my baby!"

"Is it in danger?" asked Dorothy, noticing that the child was clasped in her arms and seemed sleeping peacefully.

"Yes, indeed," said the woman, nervously. "If I should go into the house and throw my child out of the window, it would roll way down to the bottom of the hill; and then if there were a lot of tigers and bears down there, they would tear my darling babe to pieces and eat it up!"

"Are there any tigers and bears in this neighborhood?" the Wizard asked.

"I've never heard of any," admitted the woman; "but if there were—"

"Have you any idea of throwing your baby out of the window?" questioned the little man.

"None at all," she said; "but if—"

"All your troubles are due to those 'ifs'," declared the Wizard. "If you were not a Flutterbudget you wouldn't worry."

"There's another 'if'," replied the woman. "Are you a Flutterbudget, too?"

"I will be, if I stay here long," exclaimed the Wizard, nervously.

"Another 'if'!" cried the woman.

But the Wizard did not stop to argue with her. He made the Sawhorse canter all the way down the hill, and only breathed easily when they were miles away from the village.

After they had ridden in silence for a while Dorothy turned to the little man and asked:

"Do 'ifs' really make Flutterbudgets?"

"I think the 'ifs' help," he answered seriously. "Foolish fears, and worries over nothing, with a mixture of nerves and ifs, will soon make a Flutterbudget of any one."

Then there was another long silence, for all the travelers were thinking over this statement, and nearly all decided it must be true.

The country they were now passing through was everywhere tinted purple, the prevailing color of the Gillikin Country; but as the Sawhorse ascended a hill they found that upon the other side everything was of a rich yellow hue.

"Aha!" cried the Captain General; "here is the Country of the Winkies. We are just crossing the boundary line."

"Then we may be able to lunch with the Tin Woodman," announced the Wizard, joyfully.

"Must we lunch on tin?" asked Aunt Em.

"Oh, no," replied Dorothy. "Nick Chopper

knows how to feed meat people, and he will give us plenty of good things to eat, never fear. I've been to his castle before."

"Is Nick Chopper the Tin Woodman's name?" asked Uncle Henry.

"Yes; that's one of his names," answered the little girl; "and another of his names is 'Em'pror of the Winkies.' He's the King of this country, you know, but Ozma rules over all the countries of Oz."

"Does the Tin Woodman keep any Flutterbudgets or Rigmaroles at his castle?" inquired Aunt Em, uneasily.

"No, indeed," said Dorothy, positively. "He lives in a new tin castle, all full of lovely things."

"I should think it would rust," said Uncle Henry.

"He has thousands of Winkies to keep it polished for him," explained the Wizard. "His people love to do anything in their power for their beloved Emperor, so there isn't a particle of rust on all the big castle."

"I suppose they polish their Emperor, too," said Aunt Em.

"Why, some time ago he had himself nickel-plated," the Wizard answered; "so he only needs rubbing up once in a while. He's the brightest man in all the world, is dear Nick Chopper; and the kindest-hearted."

"I helped find him," said Dorothy, reflectively. "Once the Scarecrow and I found the Tin Woodman in the woods, and he was just rusted still, that time, an' no mistake. But we oiled his joints, an' got 'em good and slippery, and after that he went with us to visit the Wizard at the Em'rald City."

"Was that the time the Wizard scared you?" asked Aunt Em.

"He didn't treat us well, at first," acknowledged Dorothy; "for he made us go away and destroy the Wicked Witch. But after we found out he was only a humbug wizard we were not afraid of him."

The Wizard sighed and looked a little ashamed.

"When we try to deceive people we always

make mistakes," he said. "But I'm getting to be a real wizard now, and Glinda the Good's magic, that I am trying to practice, can never harm any one."

"You were always a good man," declared Dorothy, "even when you were a bad wizard."

"He's a good wizard now," asserted Aunt Em, looking at the little man admiringly. "The way he made those tents grow out of handkerchiefs was just wonderful! And didn't he enchant the wagon wheels so they'd find the road?"

"All the people of Oz," said the Captain General, "are very proud of their Wizard. He once made some soap-bubbles that astonished the world."

The Wizard blushed at this praise, yet it pleased him. He no longer looked sad, but seemed to have recovered his usual good humor.

The country through which they now rode was thickly dotted with farmhouses, and yellow grain waved in all the fields. Many of the Winkies could be seen working on their farms and the wild and unsettled parts of Oz were by this time left far behind.

These Winkies appeared to be happy, light-hearted folk, and all removed their caps and bowed low when the red wagon with its load of travelers passed by.

It was not long before they saw something glittering in the sunshine far ahead.

"See!" cried Dorothy; "that's the Tin Castle, Aunt Em!"

And the Sawhorse, knowing his passengers were eager to arrive, broke into a swift trot that soon brought them to their destination.

How THE TIN WOODMAN TOLD THE SAD NEWS

CHAPTER TWENTY-FOUR

THE Tin Woodman received Princess Dorothy's party with much grace and cordiality, yet the little girl decided that something must be worrying her old friend, because he was not so merry as usual.

But at first she said nothing about this, for Uncle Henry and Aunt Em were fairly bubbling over with admiration for the beautiful tin castle and its polished tin owner. So her suspicion that something unpleasant had happened was for a time forgotten.

"Where is the Scarecrow?" she asked, when they had all been ushered into the big tin drawing-room of the castle, the Sawhorse being led around to the tin stable in the rear.

"Why, our old friend has just moved into his new mansion," explained the Tin Woodman. "It has been a long time in building, although my

Winkies and many other people from all parts of the country have been busily working upon it. At last, however, it is completed, and the Scarecrow took possession of his new home just two days ago."

"I hadn't heard that he wanted a home of his own," said Dorothy. "Why doesn't he live with Ozma in the Emerald City? He used to, you know; and I thought he was happy there."

"It seems," said the Tin Woodman, "that our dear Scarecrow cannot be contented with city life, however beautiful his surroundings might be. Originally he was a farmer, for he passed his early life in a cornfield, where he was supposed to frighten away the crows."

"I know," said Dorothy, nodding. "I found him, and lifted him down from his pole."

"So now, after a long residence in the Emerald City, his tastes have turned to farm life again," continued the Tin Man. "He feels that he cannot be happy without a farm of his own, so Ozma gave him some land and every one helped him build his mansion, and now he is settled there for good."

"Who designed his house?" asked the Shaggy Man.

"I believe it was Jack Pumpkinhead, who is also a farmer," was the reply.

They were now invited to enter the tin dining

room, where luncheon was served.

Aunt Em found, to her satisfaction, that Dorothy's promise was more than fulfilled; for, although the Tin Woodman had no appetite of his own, he respected the appetites of his guests and saw that they were bountifully fed.

They passed the afternoon in wandering through the beautiful gardens and grounds of the palace. The walks were all paved with sheets of tin, brightly polished, and there were tin fountains and tin statues here and there among the trees. The flowers were mostly natural flowers and grew in the regular way; but their host showed them one flower bed which was his especial pride.

"You see, all common flowers fade and die in time," he explained, "and so there are seasons when the pretty blooms are scarce. Therefore I decided to make one tin flower bed all of tin flowers, and my workmen have created them with rare skill. Here you see tin camelias, tin marigolds, tin carnations, tin poppies and tin hollyhocks growing as naturally as if they were real."

Indeed, they were a pretty sight, and glistened under the sunlight like spun silver.

"Isn't this tin hollyhock going to seed?" asked the Wizard, bending over the flowers.

"Why, I believe it is!" exclaimed the Tin Woodman, as if surprised. "I hadn't noticed that before. But I shall plant the tin seeds and raise another bed of tin hollyhocks."

In one corner of the gardens Nick Chopper had established a fish-pond, in which they saw swimming and disporting themselves many pretty tin fishes.

"Would they bite on hooks?" asked Aunt Em, curiously.

The Tin Woodman seemed hurt at this question.

"Madam," said he, "do you suppose I would allow anyone to catch my beautiful fishes, even if they were foolish enough to bite on hooks? No, indeed! Every created thing is safe from harm in my domain, and I would as soon think of killing my little friend Dorothy as killing one of my tin fishes."

"The Emperor is very kind-hearted, ma'am," explained the Wizard. "If a fly happens to light upon his tin body he doesn't rudely brush it off, as some people might do; he asks it politely to find some other resting place."

"What does the fly do then?" enquired Aunt Em.

"Usually it begs his pardon and goes away," said the Wizard, gravely. "Flies like to be treated politely as well as other creatures, and here in Oz they understand what we say to them, and behave very nicely."

"Well," said Aunt Em, "the flies in Kansas, where I came from, don't understand anything but a swat. You have to smash 'em to make 'em behave; and it's the same way with 'skeeters. Do you have 'skeeters in Oz?"

"We have some very large mosquitoes here, which sing as beautifully as song birds," replied the Tin Woodman. "But they never bite or annoy our people, because they are well fed and taken care of. The reason they bite people in your country is because they are hungry— poor things!"

"Yes," agreed Aunt Em; "they're hungry, all right. An' they ain't very particular who they feed on. I'm glad you've got the 'skeeters educated in Oz."

That evening after dinner they were entertained by the Emperor's Tin Cornet Band, which played for them several sweet melodies. Also the Wizard did a few sleight-of-hand tricks to amuse the company; after which they all retired to their cosy tin bedrooms and slept soundly until morning.

After breakfast Dorothy said to the Tin Woodman:

"If you'll tell us which way to go we'll visit

the Scarecrow on our way home."

"I will go with you, and show you the way," replied the Emperor; "for I must journey to-day to the Emerald City."

He looked so anxious, as he said this, that the little girl asked:

"There isn't anything wrong with Ozma, is there?"

He shook his tin head.

"Not yet," said he; "but I'm afraid the time has come when I must tell you some very bad news, little friend."

"Oh, what is it?" cried Dorothy.

"Do you remember the Nome King?" asked the Tin Woodman.

"I remember him very well," she replied.

"The Nome King has not a kind heart," said the Emperor, sadly, "and he has been harboring wicked thoughts of revenge, because we once defeated him and liberated his slaves and you took away his Magic Belt. So he has ordered his Nomes to dig a long tunnel underneath the deadly desert, so that he may march his hosts right into the Emerald City. When he gets there he intends to destroy our beautiful country."

Dorothy was much surprised to hear this.

"How did Ozma find out about the tunnel?" she asked.

"She saw it in her Magic Picture."

"Of course," said Dorothy; "I might have known that. And what is she going to do?"

"I cannot tell," was the reply.

"Pooh!" cried the Yellow Hen. "We're not afraid of the Nomes. If we roll a few of our eggs down the tunnel they'll run away back home as fast as they can go."

"Why, that's true enough!" exclaimed Dorothy. "The Scarecrow once conquered all the Nome King's army with some of Billina's eggs."

"But you do not understand all of the dreadful plot," continued the Tin Woodman. "The Nome King is clever, and he knows his Nomes would run from eggs; so he has bargained with many terrible creatures to help him. These evil spirits are not afraid of eggs or anything else, and they are very powerful. So the Nome King will send them through the tunnel first, to conquer and destroy, and then the Nomes will follow after to get their share of the plunder and slaves."

They were all startled to hear this, and every face wore a troubled look.

"Is the tunnel all ready?" asked Dorothy.

"Ozma sent me word yesterday that the tunnel was all completed except for a thin crust of earth at the end. When our enemies break through this crust they will be in the gardens of the royal palace, in the heart of the Emerald

City. I offered to arm all my Winkies and march to Ozma's assistance; but she said no."

"I wonder why?" asked Dorothy.

"She answered that all the inhabitants of Oz, gathered together, were not powerful enough to fight and overcome the evil forces of the Nome King. Therefore she refuses to fight at all."

"But they will capture and enslave us, and plunder and ruin all our lovely land!" exclaimed the Wizard, greatly disturbed by this statement.

"I fear they will," said the Tin Woodman, sorrowfully. "And I also fear that those who are not fairies, such as the Wizard, and Dorothy, and her uncle and aunt, as well as Toto and Billina, will be speedily put to death by the conquerors."

"What can be done?" asked Dorothy, shud-

dering a little at the prospect of this awful fate.

"Nothing can be done!" gloomily replied the Emperor of the Winkies. "But since Ozma refuses my army I will go myself to the Emerald City. The least I may do is to perish beside my beloved Ruler."

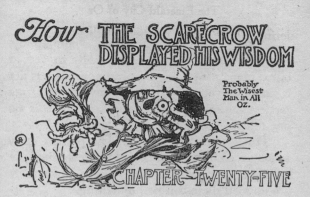

How THE SCARECROW DISPLAYED HIS WISDOM

Probably The Wisest Man in All Oz.

CHAPTER TWENTY-FIVE

THIS amazing news had saddened every heart and all were now anxious to return to the Emerald City and share Ozma's fate. So they started without loss of time, and as the road led past the Scarecrow's new mansion they determined to make a brief halt there and confer with him.

"The Scarecrow is probably the wisest man in all Oz," remarked the Tin Woodman, when they had started upon their journey. "His brains are plentiful and of excellent quality, and often he has told me things I might never have thought of myself. I must say I rely a good deal upon the Scarecrow's brains in this emergency."

The Tin Woodman rode on the front seat of the wagon, where Dorothy sat between him and the Wizard.

"Has the Scarecrow heard of Ozma's trouble?" asked the Captain General.

"I do not know, sir," was the reply.

"When I was a private," said Omby Amby, "I was an excellent army, as I fully proved in our war against the Nomes. But now there is not a single private left in our army, since Ozma made me the Captain General, so there is no one to fight and defend our lovely Ruler."

"True," said the Wizard. "The present army is composed only of officers, and the business of an officer is to order his men to fight. Since there are no men there can be no fighting."

"Poor Ozma!" whispered Dorothy, with tears in her sweet eyes. "It's dreadful to think of all her lovely fairy country being destroyed. I wonder if we couldn't manage to escape and get back to Kansas by means of the Magic Belt? And we might take Ozma with us and all work hard to get money for her, so she wouldn't be so *very* lonely and unhappy about the loss of her fairy-land."

"Do you think there would be any work for *me* in Kansas?" asked the Tin Woodman.

"If you are hollow, they might use you in a canning factory," suggested Uncle Henry. "But I can't see the use of your working for a living. You never eat or sleep or need a new suit of clothes."

"I was not thinking of myself," replied the Emperor, with dignity. "I merely wondered if

I could not help to support Dorothy and Ozma."

As they indulged in these sad plans for the future they journeyed in sight of the Scarecrow's new mansion, and even though filled with care and worry over the impending fate of Oz, Dorothy could not help a feeling of wonder at the sight she saw.

The Scarecrow's new house was shaped like an immense ear of corn. The rows of kernels were made of solid gold, and the green upon which the ear stood upright was a mass of sparkling emeralds. Upon the very top of the structure was perched a figure representing the Scarecrow himself, and upon his extended arms, as well as upon his head, were several crows carved out of ebony and having ruby eyes. You may imagine how big this ear of corn was when I tell you that a single gold kernel formed a window, swinging outward upon hinges, while a row of four kernels opened to make the front entrance. Inside there were five stories, each story being a single room.

The gardens around the mansion consisted of cornfields, and Dorothy acknowledged that the place was in all respects a very appropriate home for her good friend the Scarecrow.

"He would have been very happy here, I'm sure," she said, "if only the Nome King had left us alone. But if Oz is destroyed of course this place will be destroyed too."

"Yes," replied the Tin Woodman, "and also my beautiful tin castle, that has been my joy and pride."

"Jack Pumpkinhead's house will go too," remarked the Wizard, "as well as Professor Wogglebug's Athletic College, and Ozma's royal palace, and all our other handsome buildings."

"Yes, Oz will indeed become a desert when the Nome King gets through with it," sighed Omby Amby.

The Scarecrow came out to meet them and gave them all a hearty welcome.

"I hear you have decided always to live in the Land of Oz, after this," he said to Dorothy; "and that will delight my heart, for I have greatly disliked our frequent partings. But why are you all so downcast?"

"Have you heard the news?" asked the Tin Woodman.

"No news to make me sad," replied the Scarecrow.

Then Nick Chopper told his friend of the Nome King's tunnel, and how the evil creatures of the North had allied themselves with the underground monarch for the purpose of conquering and destroying Oz. "Well," said the Scarecrow, "it certainly looks bad for Ozma, and all of us. But I believe it is wrong to worry over anything before it happens. It is surely time enough to be sad when our country is despoiled and our people made slaves. So let us not deprive ourselves of the few happy hours remaining to us."

"Ah! that is real wisdom," declared the Shaggy Man, approvingly. "After we become really unhappy we shall regret these few hours that are left to us, unless we enjoy them to the utmost."

"Nevertheless," said the Scarecrow, "I shall go with you to the Emerald City and offer Ozma my services."

"She says we can do nothing to oppose our enemies," announced the Tin Woodman.

"And doubtless she is right, sir," answered the Scarecrow. "Still, she will appreciate our sympathy, and it is the duty of Ozma's friends to stand by her side when the final disaster occurs."

He then led them into his queer mansion and showed them the beautiful rooms in all the five stories. The lower room was a grand reception hall, with a hand-organ in one corner. This instrument the Scarecrow, when alone, could turn to amuse himself, as he was very fond of music. The walls were hung with white silk, upon which flocks of black crows were embroidered in black diamonds. Some of the chairs were made in the shape of big crows and upholstered with cushions of corn-colored silk.

The second story contained a fine banquet room, where the Scarecrow might entertain his guests, and the three stories above that were bedchambers exquisitely furnished and decorated.

"From these rooms," said the Scarecrow, proudly, "one may obtain fine views of the surrounding cornfields. The corn I grow is always husky, and I call the ears my regiments, because they have so many kernels. Of course I cannot ride my cobs, but I really don't care shucks about that. Taken altogether, my farm will stack up with any in the neighborhood."

The visitors partook of some light refreshment and then hurried away to resume the road to the Emerald City. The Scarecrow found a seat in the wagon between Omby Amby and the Shaggy Man, and his weight did not add much to the load because he was stuffed with straw.

"You will notice I have one oat-field on my property," he remarked, as they drove away. "Oat-straw is, I have found, the best of all straws to re-stuff myself with when my interior gets musty or out of shape."

"Are you able to re-stuff yourself without help?" asked Aunt Em. "I should think that after the straw was taken out of you there wouldn't be anything left but your clothes."

"You are almost correct, madam," he answered. "My servants do the stuffing, under my direction. For my head, in which are my excellent brains, is a bag tied at the bottom. My face is neatly painted upon one side of the bag, as you may see. My head does not need re-stuffing, as my body does, for all that it requires is to have the face touched up with fresh paint occasionally."

It was not far from the Scarecrow's mansion to the farm of Jack Pumpkinhead, and when they arrived there both Uncle Henry and Aunt Em were much impressed. The farm was one vast pumpkin field, and some of the pumpkins were of enormous size. In one of them, which had been neatly hollowed out, Jack himself lived, and he declared that it was a very comfortable residence. The reason he grew so many pumpkins was in order that he might change his head as often as it became wrinkled or threatened to spoil.

The pumpkin-headed man welcomed his visitors joyfully and offered them several delicious pumpkin pies to eat.

"I don't indulge in pumpkin pies myself, for two reasons," he said. "One reason is that were I to eat pumpkins I would become a cannibal, and the other reason is that I never eat, not being hollow inside."

"Very good reasons," agreed the Scarecrow.

They told Jack Pumpkinhead the dreadful news about the Nome King, and he decided to go with them to the Emerald City and help comfort Ozma.

"I had expected to live here in ease and comfort for many centuries," said Jack, dolefully; "but of course if the Nome King destroys everything in Oz I shall be destroyed too. Really, it seems too bad, doesn't it?"

They were soon on their journey again, and so swiftly did the Sawhorse draw the wagon over the smooth roads that before twilight fell they had reached the royal palace in the Emerald City, and were at their journey's end.

How OZMA REFUSED TO FIGHT FOR HER KINGDOM

CHAPTER TWENTY-SIX

OZMA was in her rose garden picking a bouquet when the party arrived, and she greeted all her old and new friends as smilingly and sweetly as ever.

Dorothy's eyes were full of tears as she kissed the lovely Ruler of Oz, and she whispered to her:

"Oh, Ozma, Ozma! I'm *so* sorry!"

Ozma seemed surprised.

"Sorry for what, Dorothy?" she asked.

"For all your trouble about the Nome King," was the reply.

Ozma laughed with genuine amusement.

"Why, that has not troubled me a bit, dear Princess," she replied. Then, looking around at the sad faces of her friends, she added: "Have you all been worrying about this tunnel?"

"We have!" they exclaimed in a chorus.

"Well, perhaps it is more serious than I imagined," admitted the fair Ruler; "but I haven't given the matter much thought. After dinner we will all meet together and talk it over."

So they went to their rooms and prepared for dinner, and Dorothy dressed herself in her prettiest gown and put on her coronet, for she thought that this might be the last time she would ever appear as a Princess of Oz.

The Scarecrow, the Tin Woodman and Jack Pumpkinhead all sat at the dinner table, although none of them was made so he could eat. Usually they served to enliven the meal with their merry talk, but to-night all seemed strangely silent and uneasy.

As soon as the dinner was finished Ozma led the company to her own private room in which hung the Magic Picture. When they had seated themselves the Scarecrow was the first to speak.

"Is the Nome King's tunnel finished, Ozma?" he asked.

"It was completed to-day," she replied. "They have built it right under my palace grounds, and it ends in front of the Forbidden Fountain. Nothing but a crust of earth remains to separate our enemies from us, and when they march here they will easily break through this crust and rush upon us."

"Who will assist the Nome King?" inquired the Scarecrow.

"The Whimsies, the Growleywogs and the Phanfasms," she replied. "I watched to-day in my Magic Picture the messengers whom the Nome King sent to all these people to summon them to assemble in his great caverns."

"Let us see what they are doing now," suggested the Tin Woodman.

So Ozma wished to see the Nome King's cavern, and at once the landscape faded from the Magic Picture and was replaced by the scene then being enacted in the jeweled cavern of King Roquat.

A wild and startling scene it was which the Oz people beheld.

Before the Nome King stood the Chief of the Whimsies and the Grand Gallipoot of the Growleywogs, surrounded by their most skillful generals. Very fierce and powerful they looked, so that even the Nome King and General Guph, who stood beside his master, seemed a bit fearful in the presence of their allies.

Now a still more formidable creature entered the cavern. It was the First and Foremost of the Phanfasms and he proudly sat down in King Roquat's own throne and demanded the right to lead his forces through the tunnel in advance of all the others. The First and Foremost now appeared to all eyes in his hairy skin and the bear's head. What his real form was even Roquat did not know.

Through the arches leading into the vast series of caverns that lay beyond the throne room of King Roquat, could be seen ranks upon ranks of the invaders—thousands of Phanfasms, Growleywogs and Whimsies standing in serried lines, while behind them were massed the thousands upon thousands of General Guph's own army of Nomes.

"Listen!" whispered Ozma. "I think we can hear what they are saying."

So they kept still and listened.

"Is all ready?" demanded the First and Foremost, haughtily.

"The tunnel is finally completed," replied General Guph.

"How long will it take us to march to the Emerald City?" asked the Grand Gallipoot of the Growleywogs.

"If we start at midnight," replied the Nome King, "we shall arrive at the Emerald City by daybreak. Then, while all the Oz people are sleeping, we will capture them and make them our slaves. After that we will destroy the city itself and march through the Land of Oz, burning and devastating as we go."

"Good!" cried the First and Foremost. "When we get through with Oz it will be a desert wilderness. Ozma shall be my slave."

"She shall be *my* slave!" shouted the Grand Gallipoot, angrily.

"We'll decide that by and by," said King Roquat, hastily. "Don't let us quarrel now, friends. First let us conquer Oz, and then we will divide the spoils of war in a satisfactory manner."

The First and Foremost smiled wickedly; but he only said:

"I and my Phanfasms go first, for nothing on earth can oppose our power."

They all agreed to that, knowing the Phanfasms to be the mightiest of the combined forces. King Roquat now invited them to attend a banquet he had prepared, where they might occupy themselves in eating and drinking until midnight arrived.

As they had now seen and heard all of the plot against them that they cared to, Ozma allowed her Magic Picture to fade away. Then she turned to her friends and said:

"Our enemies will be here sooner than I expected. What do you advise me to do?"

"It is now too late to assemble our people," said the Tin Woodman, despondently. "If you had allowed me to arm and drill my Winkies we might have put up a good fight and destroyed many of our enemies before we were conquered."

"The Munchkins are good fighters, too," said Omby Amby; "and so are the Gillikins."

"But I do not wish to fight," declared Ozma, firmly. "No one has the right to destroy any living creatures, however evil they may be, or to hurt them or make them unhappy. I will not fight—even to save my kingdom."

"The Nome King is not so particular," remarked the Scarecrow. "He intends to destroy us all and ruin our beautiful country."

"Because the Nome King intends to do evil is no excuse for my doing the same," replied Ozma.

"Self-preservation is the first law of nature," quoted the Shaggy Man.

"True," she said, readily. "I would like to discover a plan to save ourselves without fighting."

That seemed a hopeless task to them, but realizing that Ozma was determined not to fight, they tried to think of some means that might promise escape.

"Couldn't we bribe our enemies, by giving them a lot of emeralds and gold?" asked Jack Pumpkinhead.

"No, because they believe they are able to take everything we have," replied the Ruler.

"I have thought of something," said Dorothy.

"What is it, dear?" asked Ozma.

"Let us use the Magic Belt to wish all of us in Kansas. We will put some emeralds in our pockets, and can sell them in Topeka for enough to pay off the mortgage on Uncle Henry's farm. Then we can all live together and be happy."

"A clever idea!" exclaimed the Scarecrow.

"Kansas is a very good country. I've been there," said the Shaggy Man.

"That seems to me an excellent plan," approved the Tin Woodman.

"No!" said Ozma, decidedly. "Never will I desert my people and leave them to so cruel a fate. I will use the Magic Belt to send the rest of you to Kansas, if you wish, but if my beloved country must be destroyed and my people enslaved I will remain and share their fate."

"Quite right," asserted the Scarecrow, sighing. "I will remain with you."

"And so will I," declared the Tin Woodman and the Shaggy Man and Jack Pumpkinhead, in turn. Tiktok, the machine man, also said he intended to stand by Ozma. "For," said he, "I should be of no use at all in Kansas."

"For my part," announced Dorothy, gravely, "if the Ruler of Oz must not desert her people, a Princess of Oz has no right to run away, either. I'm willing to become a slave with the rest of you; so all we can do with the Magic Belt is to use it to send Uncle Henry and Aunt Em back to Kansas."

"I've been a slave all my life," Aunt Em replied, with considerable cheerfulness, "and so has Henry. I guess we won't go back to Kansas, anyway. I'd rather take my chances with the rest of you."

Ozma smiled upon them all gratefully.

"There is no need to despair just yet," she said. "I'll get up early to-morrow morning and be at the Forbidden Fountain when the fierce warriors break through the crust of earth. I will speak to them pleasantly and perhaps they won't be so very bad, after all."

"Why do they call it the Forbidden Fountain?" asked Dorothy, thoughtfully.

"Don't you know, dear?" returned Ozma, surprised.

"No," said Dorothy. "Of course I've seen the fountain in the palace grounds, ever since I first came to Oz; and I've read the sign which says: 'All Persons are Forbidden to Drink at this Fountain.' But I never knew *why* they were forbidden. The water seems clear and sparkling and it bubbles up in a golden basin all the time."

"That water," declared Ozma, gravely, "is the most dangerous thing in all the Land of Oz. It is the Water of Oblivion."

"What does that mean?" asked Dorothy.

"Whoever drinks at the Forbidden Fountain at once forgets everything he has ever known," Ozma asserted.

"It wouldn't be a bad way to forget our troubles," suggested Uncle Henry.

"That is true; but you would forget everything else, and become as ignorant as a baby," returned Ozma.

"Does it make one crazy?" asked Dorothy.

"No; it only makes one forget," replied the girl Ruler. "It is said that once—long, long ago—a wicked King ruled Oz, and made himself and all his people very miserable and unhappy. So Glinda, the Good Sorceress, placed this fountain here, and the King drank of its water and forgot all his wickedness. His mind became innocent and vacant, and when he learned the things of life again they were all good things. But the people remembered how wicked their King had been, and were still afraid of him. Therefore he made them all drink of the Water of Oblivion and forget everything they had known, so that they became as simple and innocent as their King. After that they all grew wise together, and their wisdom was good, so that peace and happiness reigned in the land. But for fear some one might drink of the water again, and in an instant forget all he had learned, the King put that sign upon the fountain, where it has remained for many centuries up to this very day."

They had all listened intently to Ozma's story, and when she finished speaking there was a long period of silence while all thought upon the curious magical power of the Water of Oblivion.

Finally the Scarecrow's painted face took on a broad smile that stretched the cloth as far as it would go.

"How thankful I am," he said, "that I have such an excellent assortment of brains!"

"I gave you the best brains I ever mixed," declared the Wizard, with an air of pride.

"You did, indeed!" agreed the Scarecrow, "and they work so splendidly that they have found a way to save Oz—to save us all!"

"I'm glad to hear that," said the Wizard. "We never needed saving more than we do just now."

"Do you mean to say you can save us from those awful Phanfasms, and Growleywogs and Whimsies?" asked Dorothy eagerly.

"I'm sure of it, my dear," asserted the Scarecrow, still smiling genially.

"Tell us how!" cried the Tin Woodman.

"Not now," said the Scarecrow. "You may all go to bed, and I advise you to forget your worries just as completely as if you had drunk of the Water of Oblivion in the Forbidden Fountain. I'm going to stay here and tell my plan to Ozma alone, but if you will all be at the Forbidden Fountain at daybreak, you'll see how easily we will save the kingdom when our enemies break through the crust of earth and come from the tunnel."

So they went away and left the Scarecrow and Ozma alone; but Dorothy could not sleep a wink all night.

"He is only a Scarecrow," she said to herself, "and I'm not sure that his mixed brains are as clever as he thinks they are."

But she knew that if the Scarecrow's plan failed they were all lost; so she tried to have faith in him.

How THE FIERCE WARRIORS INVADED OZ

CHAPTER TWENTY-SEVEN

THE Nome King and his terrible allies sat at the banquet table until midnight. There was much quarreling between the Growleywogs and Phanfasms, and one of the wee-headed Whimsies got angry at General Guph and choked him until he nearly stopped breathing. Yet no one was seriously hurt, and the Nome King felt much relieved when the clock struck twelve and they all sprang up and seized their weapons.

"Aha!" shouted the First and Foremost. "Now to conquer the Land of Oz!"

He marshaled his Phanfasms in battle array and at his word of command they marched into the tunnel and began the long journey through it to the Emerald City. The First and Foremost intended to take all the treasures in Oz for himself; to kill all who could be killed and enslave the rest; to destroy and lay waste the whole country, and afterward to conquer and enslave the Nomes, the Growleywogs and the Whimsies. And he knew his power was sufficient to enable him to do all these things easily.

Next marched into the tunnel the army of gigantic Growleywogs, with their Grand Gallipoot at their head. They were dreadful beings, indeed, and longed to get to Oz that they might begin to pilfer and destroy. The Grand Gallipoot was a little afraid of the First and Foremost, but had a cunning plan to murder or destroy that powerful being and secure the wealth of Oz for himself. Mighty little of the plunder would the Nome King get, thought the Grand Gallipoot.

The Chief of the Whimsies now marched his false-headed forces into the tunnel. In his wicked little head was a plot to destroy both the First and Foremost and the Grand Gallipoot. He intended to let them conquer Oz, since they insisted on going first; but he would afterward treacherously destroy them, as well as King Roquat, and keep all the slaves and treasure of Ozma's kingdom for himself.

After all his dangerous allies had marched into the tunnel the Nome King and General Guph started to follow them, at the head of fifty thousand Nomes, all fully armed.

"Guph," said the King, "those creatures ahead of us mean mischief. They intend to get everything for themselves and leave us nothing."

"I know," replied the General; "but they are not as clever as they think they are. When you get the Magic Belt you must at once wish the Whimsies and Growleywogs and the Phanfasms all back into their own countries—and the Belt will surely take them there."

"Good!" cried the King. "An excellent plan, Guph. I'll do it. While they are conquering Oz I'll get the Magic Belt, and then only the Nomes will remain to ravage the country."

So you see there was only one thing that all were agreed upon—that Oz should be destroyed.

On, on, on the vast ranks of invaders marched, filling the tunnel from side to side. With a steady tramp, tramp, they advanced, every step taking them nearer to the beautiful Emerald City.

"Nothing can save the Land of Oz!" thought the First and Foremost, scowling until his bear face was as black as the tunnel.

"The Emerald City is as good as destroyed already!" muttered the Grand Gallipoot, shaking his war club fiercely.

"In a few hours Oz will be a desert!" said the Chief of the Whimsies, with an evil laugh.

"My dear Guph," remarked the Nome King to his General, "at last my vengeance upon Ozma of Oz and her people is about to be accomplished."

"You are right!" declared the General. "Ozma is surely lost."

And now the First and Foremost, who was in advance and nearing the Emerald City, began to cough and to sneeze.

"This tunnel is terribly dusty," he growled, angrily. "I'll punish that Nome King for not having it swept clean. My throat and eyes are getting full of dust and I'm as thirsty as a fish!"

The Grand Gallipoot was coughing too, and his throat was parched and dry.

"What a dusty place!" he cried. "I'll be glad when we reach Oz, where we can get a drink."

"Who has any water?" asked the Whimsie Chief, gasping and choking. But none of his followers carried a drop of water, so he hastened on to get through the dusty tunnel to the Land of Oz.

"Where did all this dust come from?" demanded General Guph, trying hard to swallow but finding his throat so dry he couldn't.

"I don't know," answered the Nome King. "I've been in the tunnel every day while it was being built, but I never noticed any dust before."

"Let's hurry!" cried the General. "I'd give half the gold in Oz for a drink of water."

The dust grew thicker and thicker, and the throats and eyes and noses of the invaders were filled with it. But not one halted or turned back. They hurried forward more fierce and vengeful than ever.

How They Drank at the Forbidden Fountain

How THEY DRANK AT THE FORBIDDEN FOUNTAIN

CHAPTER TWENTY-EIGHT

THE Scarecrow had no need to sleep; neither had the Tin Woodman or Tiktok or Jack Pumpkinhead. So they all wandered out into the palace grounds and stood beside the sparkling water of the Forbidden Fountain until daybreak. During this time they indulged in occasional conversation.

"Nothing could make me forget what I know," remarked the Scarecrow, gazing into the fountain, "for I cannot drink the Water of Oblivion or water of any kind. And I am glad that this is so, for I consider my wisdom unexcelled."

"You are cer-tain-ly ve-ry wise," agreed Tiktok. "For my part, I can on-ly think by ma-chin-er-y, so I do not pre-tend to know as much as you do."

"My tin brains are very bright, but that is all

I claim for them," said Nick Chopper, modestly. "Yet I do not aspire to being very wise, for I have noticed that the happiest people are those who do not let their brains oppress them."

"Mine never worry me," Jack Pumpkinhead acknowledged. "There are many seeds of thought in my head, but they do not sprout easily. I am glad that it is so, for if I occupied my days in thinking I should have no time for anything else."

In this cheery mood they passed the hours until the first golden streaks of dawn appeared in the sky. Then Ozma joined them, as fresh and lovely as ever and robed in one of her prettiest gowns.

"Our enemies have not yet arrived," said the Scarecrow, after greeting affectionately the sweet and girlish Ruler.

"They will soon be here," she said, "for I have just glanced at my Magic Picture, and have seen them coughing and choking with the dust in the tunnel."

"Oh, is there dust in the tunnel?" asked the Tin Woodman.

"Yes; Ozma placed it there by means of the Magic Belt," explained the Scarecrow, with one of his broad smiles.

Then Dorothy came to them, Uncle Henry and Aunt Em following close after her. The little girl's eyes were heavy because she had had a sleepless and anxious night. Toto walked by her side, but the little dog's spirits were very much subdued. Billina, who was always up by daybreak, was not long in joining the group by the fountain.

The Wizard and the Shaggy Man next arrived, and soon after appeared Omby Amby, dressed in his best uniform.

"There lies the tunnel," said Ozma, pointing to a part of the ground just before the Forbidden Fountain, "and in a few moments the dreadful invaders will break through the earth and swarm over the land. Let us all stand on the other side of the Fountain and watch to see what happens."

At once they followed her suggestion and moved around the fountain of the Water of Oblivion. There they stood silent and expectant until the earth beyond gave way with a sudden crash and up leaped the powerful form of the First and Foremost, followed by all his grim warriors.

As the leader sprang forward his gleaming eyes caught the play of the fountain and he rushed toward it and drank eagerly of the sparkling water. Many of the other Phanfasms drank, too, in order to clear their dry and dusty throats. Then they stood around and looked at one another with simple, wondering smiles.

The First and Foremost saw Ozma and her companions beyond the fountain, but instead of making an effort to capture her he merely stared at her in pleased admiration of her beauty—for he had forgotten where he was and why he had come there.

But now the Grand Gallipoot arrived, rushing from the tunnel with a hoarse cry of mingled rage and thirst. He too saw the fountain and hastened to drink of its forbidden waters. The other Growleywogs were not slow to follow suit, and even before they had finished drinking the Chief of the Whimsies and his people came to push them away, while they one and all cast off their false heads that they might slake their thirst at the fountain.

When the Nome King and General Guph arrived they both made a dash to drink, but the General was so mad with thirst that he knocked his King over, and while Roquat lay sprawling upon the ground the General drank heartily of the Water of Oblivion.

This rude act of his General made the Nome King so angry that for a moment he forgot he was thirsty and rose to his feet to glare upon the group of terrible warriors he had brought here to assist him. He saw Ozma and her people, too, and yelled out:

"Why don't you capture them? Why don't you conquer Oz, you idiots? Why do you stand there like a lot of dummies?"

But the great warriors had become like little children. They had forgotten all their enmity against Ozma and against Oz. They had even forgotten who they themselves were, or why they were in this strange and beautiful country. As for the Nome King, they did not recognize him, and wondered who he was.

The sun came up and sent its flood of silver rays to light the faces of the invaders. The frowns and scowls and evil looks were all gone. Even the most monstrous of the creatures there assembled smiled innocently and seemed lighthearted and content merely to be alive.

Not so with Roquat, the Nome King. He had not drunk from the Forbidden Fountain and all his former rage against Ozma and Dorothy now inflamed him as fiercely as ever. The sight of General Guph babbling like a happy child and playing with his hands in the cool waters of the fountain astonished and maddened Red Roquat. Seeing that his terrible allies and his own General refused to act, the Nome King turned to order his great army of Nomes to advance from the tunnel and seize the helpless Oz people.

But the Scarecrow suspected what was in the King's mind and spoke a word to the Tin Woodman. Together they ran at Roquat and grabbing him up tossed him into the great basin of the fountain.

The Nome King's body was round as a ball, and it bobbed up and down in the Water of Oblivion while he spluttered and screamed with

fear lest he should drown. And when he cried out his mouth filled with water, which ran down his throat, so that straightway he forgot all he had formerly known just as completely as had all the other invaders.

Ozma and Dorothy could not refrain from laughing to see their dreaded enemies become as harmless as babes. There was no danger now that Oz would be destroyed. The only question remaining to solve was how to get rid of this horde of intruders.

The Shaggy Man kindly pulled the Nome King out of the fountain and set him upon his thin legs. Roquat was dripping wet, but he chattered and laughed and wanted to drink more of the water. No thought of injuring any person was now in his mind.

Before he left the tunnel he had commanded his fifty thousand Nomes to remain there until he ordered them to advance, as he wished to give his allies time to conquer Oz before he appeared with his own army. Ozma did not wish all these Nomes to overrun her land, so she advanced to King Roquat and taking his hand in her own said gently:

"Who are you? What is your name?"

"I don't know," he replied, smiling at her. "Who are you, my dear?"

"My name is Ozma," she said; "and your name is Roquat."

"Oh, is it?" he replied, seeming pleased.

"Yes; you are King of the Nomes," she said.

"Ah; I wonder what the Nomes are!" returned the King, as if puzzled.

"They are underground elves, and that tunnel over there is full of them," she answered. "You have a beautiful cavern at the other end of the tunnel, so you must go to your Nomes and say: 'March home!' Then follow after them and in time you will reach the pretty cavern where you live."

The Nome King was much pleased to learn this, for he had forgotten he had a cavern. So he went to the tunnel and said to his army: "March home!" At once the Nomes turned and marched back through the tunnel, and the King

followed after them, laughing with delight to find his orders so readily obeyed.

The Wizard went to General Guph, who was trying to count his fingers, and told him to follow the Nome King, who was his master. Guph meekly obeyed, and so all the Nomes quitted the Land of Oz forever.

But there were still the Phanfasms and Whimsies and Growleywogs standing around in groups, and they were so many that they filled the gardens and trampled upon the flowers and grass because they did not know that the tender plants would be injured by their clumsy feet. But in all other respects they were perfectly harmless and played together like children or gazed with pleasure upon the pretty sights of the royal gardens.

After counseling with the Scarecrow Ozma sent Omby Amby to the palace for the Magic Belt, and when the Captain General returned with it the Ruler of Oz at once clasped the precious Belt around her waist.

"I wish all these strange people—the Whimsies and the Growleywogs and the Phanfasms—safe back in their own homes!" she said.

It all happened in a twinkling, for of course the wish was no sooner spoken than it was granted.

All the hosts of the invaders were gone, and only the trampled grass showed that they had ever been in the Land of Oz.

How GLINDA WORKED A MAGIC·SPELL

CHAPTER TWENTY-NINE

"THAT was better than fighting," said Ozma, when all our friends were assembled in the palace after the exciting events of the morning; and each and every one agreed with her.

"No one was hurt," said the Wizard delightly.

"And no one hurt us," added Aunt Em.

"But, best of all," said Dorothy, "the wicked people have all forgotten their wickedness, and will not wish to hurt any one after this."

"True, Princess," declared the Shaggy Man. "It seems to me that to have reformed all those evil characters is more important than to have saved Oz."

"Nevertheless," remarked the Scarecrow, "I am glad Oz is saved. I can now go back to my new mansion and live happily."

"And I am glad and grateful that my pumpkin farm is saved," said Jack.

"For my part," added the Tin Woodman, "I cannot express my joy that my lovely tin castle is not to be demolished by wicked enemies."

"Still," said Tiktok, "o-ther en-e-mies may come to Oz some day."

"Why do you allow your clock-work brains to interrupt our joy?" asked Omby Amby, frowning at the machine man.

"I say what I am wound up to say," answered Tiktok.

"And you are right," declared Ozma. "I myself have been thinking of this very idea, and it seems to me there are entirely too many ways for people to get to the Land of Oz. We used to think the deadly desert that surrounds us was enough protection; but that is no longer the case. The Wizard and Dorothy have both come here through the air, and I am told the earth people have invented airships that can fly anywhere they wish them to go."

"Why, sometimes they do, and sometimes they don't," asserted Dorothy.

"But in time the airships may cause us trouble," continued Ozma, "for if the earth folk learn how to manage them we would be overrun with visitors who would ruin our lovely, secluded fairyland."

"That is true enough," agreed the Wizard.

"Also the desert fails to protect us in other ways," Ozma went on, thoughtfully. "Johnny Dooit once made a sandboat that sailed across it, and the Nome King made a tunnel under it. So I believe something ought to be done to cut us off from the rest of the world entirely, so that no one in the future will ever be able to intrude upon us."

"How will you do that?" asked the Scarecrow.

"I do not know; but in some way I am sure it can be accomplished. To-morrow I will make a journey to the castle of Glinda the Good, and ask her advice."

"May I go with you?" asked Dorothy, eagerly.

"Of course, my dear Princess; and also I invite any of our friends here who would like to undertake the journey."

They all declared they wished to accompany their girl Ruler, for this was indeed an important mission, since the future of the Land of Oz to a great extent depended upon it. So Ozma gave orders to her servants to prepare for the journey on the morrow.

That day she watched her Magic Picture, and when it showed her that all the Nomes had returned through the tunnel to their underground caverns, Ozma used the Magic Belt to close up the tunnel, so that the earth underneath the desert sands became as solid as it was before the Nomes began to dig.

Early the following morning a gay cavalcade set out to visit the famous Sorceress, Glinda the Good. Ozma and Dorothy rode in a chariot drawn by the Cowardly Lion and the Hungry Tiger, while the Sawhorse drew the red wagon in which rode the rest of the party.

With hearts light and free from care they traveled merrily along through the lovely and fascinating Land of Oz, and in good season reached the stately castle in which resided the Sorceress.

Glinda knew that they were coming.

"I have been reading about you in my Magic Book," she said, as she greeted them in her gracious way.

"What is your Magic Book like?" inquired Aunt Em, curiously.

"It is a record of everything that happens," replied the Sorceress. "As soon as an event takes place, anywhere in the world, it is immediately found printed in my Magic Book. So when I read its pages I am well informed."

"Did it tell how our enemies drank the Water of 'Blivion?" asked Dorothy.

"Yes, my dear; it told all about it. And also it told me you were all coming to my castle, and why."

"Then," said Ozma, "I suppose you know what is in my mind, and that I am seeking a way to prevent any one in the future from discovering the Land of Oz."

"Yes; I know that. And while you were on your journey I have thought of a way to accomplish your desire. For it seems to me unwise to allow too many outside people to come here. Dorothy, with her uncle and aunt, has now returned to Oz to live always, and there is no reason why we should leave any way open for others to travel uninvited to our fairyland. Let us make it impossible for any one ever to communicate with us in any way, after this. Then we may live peacefully and contentedly."

"Your advice is wise," returned Ozma. "I thank you, Glinda, for your promise to assist me."

"But how can you do it?" asked Dorothy. "How can you keep every one from ever finding Oz?"

"By making our country invisible to all eyes but our own," replied the Sorceress, smiling. "I have a magic charm powerful enough to accomplish that wonderful feat, and now that we have been warned of our danger by the Nome King's invasion, I believe we must not hesitate to separate ourselves forever from all the rest of the world."

"I agree with you," said the Ruler of Oz.

"Won't it make any difference to us?" asked Dorothy, doubtfully.

"No, my dear," Glinda answered, assuringly. "We shall still be able to see each other and everything in the Land of Oz. It won't affect us at all; but those who fly through the air over our country will look down and see nothing at all. Those who come to the edge of the desert, or try to cross it, will catch no glimpse of Oz, or know in what direction it lies. No one will try to tunnel to us again because we cannot be seen and therefore cannot be found. In other words, the Land of Oz will entirely disappear from the knowledge of the rest of the world."

"That's all right," said Dorothy, cheerfully.

"You may make Oz invis'ble as soon as you please, for all I care."

"It is already invisible," Glinda stated. "I knew Ozma's wishes, and performed the Magic Spell before you arrived."

Ozma seized the hand of the Sorceress and pressed it gratefully.

"Thank you!" she said.

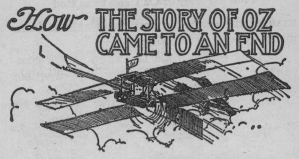

How THE STORY OF OZ CAME TO AN END

CHAPTER THIRTY

THE writer of these Oz stories has received a little note from Princess Dorothy of Oz which, for a time, has made him feel rather discontented. The note was written on a broad white feather from a stork's wing, and it said:

> *"You will never hear anything more about Oz, because we are now cut off forever from all the rest of the world. But Toto and I will always love you and all the other children who love us.*
> "DOROTHY GALE."

This seemed to me too bad, at first, for Oz is a very interesting fairyland. Still, we have no right to feel grieved, for we have had enough of the history of the Land of Oz to fill six story books, and from its quaint people and their strange adventures we have been able to learn many useful and amusing things.

So good luck to little Dorothy and her companions. May they live long in their invisible country and be very happy!

THE END